Praise for *The Ancient Minstrel*

A *New York Times*, GLIBA, MIBA, NCIBA, PNBA, SCIBA Bestseller

An Amazon Editors' Best Book of the Month

"As in his 1988 novel *Dalva*, which many consider his finest work, Harrison's handling of a woman's perspective is excellent . . . beautiful . . . Harrison, who died pen in hand at his desk writing a poem, clearly retained use of his lyrical powers until the very end . . . The quality of work he's left us is unassailable."
—*Missoula Independent*

"Jim Harrison's prose is gorgeous, illuminating. The simple language slides into your head but resonates there because of its subtle and efficient arrangement . . . Some of his grand, sweeping sentences, in the style of Chekhov or Flaubert, contain entire stories . . . But then these novelistic sentences shift to the immediate, the concrete, the matter-of-fact, as an anodyne against grandiosity."
—*Arts Fuse*

"Harrison will probably be remembered best for his novellas . . . His prose was muscular, shorn of the extraneous, and could hit the reader like a punch between the eyes . . . What is so touching and so wonderful about *The Ancient Minstrel* is the prose. It remains as strong as ever."
—*Smoky Mountain News*

"Memoir in general has always been a pretty slippery genre, and whether the narrator of *The Ancient Minstrel* is the real Jim Harrison or some carefully constructed performance might just be a distinction without a difference. Whoever he is, he tells a fine story." —*Tampa Bay Times*

"Harrison, who proved himself master of the novella with works like *Legends of the Fall*, serves up a trio full of his trademark humor and insight." —*Boston Globe*

"An author of fiction, poetry, essays, and memoir that—in their contagious vitality, their celebratory and compassionate explorations of the pleasures and pains that come with being alive on this rich earth—have done more to heal, inspire, and delight me than the work of any other artist . . . Like so much of his other work, [*The Ancient Minstrel*] alleviated my sadness." —*The Millions*

"Jim Harrison's novellas are always on point . . . One of the Midwest's best. The man is legend." —*Book Riot*

"An ascended master of the form returns to the novella . . . [Harrison] writes with his customary rough grace and bodhisattva wisdom, whether comically treating sexual improprieties or reflecting deeply on the meaning of life . . . Grand entertainments all and a pleasure." —*Kirkus Reviews* (starred review)

"*The Ancient Minstrel* satisfies like an after-dinner drink. *Eggs* is my favorite because Harrison is adept at writing female characters with agency, as his 1988 novel *Dalva*

illustrates. I also enjoyed the title story for its wry humor and its faux-memoir style . . . [*The Ancient Minstrel*] is for anyone who has ever dared to escape the private cell of the mind."
                                                   —*Arizona Daily Sun*

"Harrison . . . still has one of the most companionable voices in American letters."   —*Publishers Weekly*

"The whole of *The Ancient Minstrel* is redolent of the so-called writing life . . . [*Eggs* is] full of grace and humor . . . *The Ancient Minstrel* is certainly a fitting marker for Harrison's lifework."   —*New West*

"One of our Grand Old Writers, Harrison has a way with novellas . . . and these pieces are classic."   —*Library Journal*

"The book is great . . . A blend of humor (much of it bawdy), sex (ditto) and observations on the human condition that verge on the profound."   —*Washington Times*

"Harrison needles his own myth from start to now . . . Jim Harrison's characters in *The Ancient Minstrel* as before, demonstrate how Michigan's mythology is intimately— and intricately—woven. Good reading."
                                              —*Petoskey News Review*

The Ancient
Minstrel

Also by Jim Harrison

JIM HARRISON

The Ancient Minstrel

Novellas

Grove Press
New York

Published simultaneously in Canada
Printed in the United States of America

First Grove Atlantic hardcover edition: March 2016

First Grove Atlantic paperback edition: March 2017

ISBN 978-0-8021-2634-4
eISBN 978-0-8021-9021-5

Grove Press
An imprint of Grove Atlantic
154 West 14th Street
New York, NY 10011

Distributed by Publishers Group West

groveatlantic.com

17 18 19 20   10 9 8 7 6 5 4 3 2 1

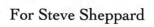

For Steve Sheppard

Contents

The Ancient Minstrel

Author's Note

Some years ago when I was verging on sixty years and feeling poignantly the threat of death I actually said to myself, "Time to write a memoir." So I did. Time told another story and over fifteen years later I'm still not dead, a fine surprise for a poet who presumed he'd die young in a pile on the house floor, or perhaps near the usual fountain in Rome, or withering to nothing in a garret in Paris torturously located above a bistro so I could smell food I couldn't afford to buy. I choke on a fishbone I found in the garbage, and the violent coughing and hemorrhaging kill me by dawn, still sprawled in the alley after a night of chilly rain. The shivering likely kept me alive for the night. A lovely jogger in green shorts discovers me and stands above my head, leaning over and looking for life signs of which there are none except a flickering right eye. The left eye was blind since childhood. It occurs to me that looking up at her winsome crotch I was born and am dying between a woman's legs. How appropriate because this locale has drawn a fair amount of attention in my life.

I don't regret waiting on illusions because that seems the fairness of living. In fact I spent a month trying to figure out whether I should call this novella "The Ancient Minstrel" or "The Ancient Mongrel." Both are apt whether you are showing off for pay or doing your brilliant dog tricks for pay. Mongrels are especially similar to writers. The parentage of the arts is often lost to history, or the matter has evoked dishonesty. Who cares about your noble ancestry when all of the proof is on the page? I studied Dostoyevsky and Faulkner very hard but don't see any evidence in my own work.

To be honest, which often I am not, when I began, my family insisted on being left out. My wife led the charge knowing altogether too well the fables of a writer. A friend, a successful novelist, had written a memoir that included information about his wife's affairs, affairs which in fact didn't exist but he included to absolve his own behavior. I admitted to myself that the same was not beyond me though I would veil it all as jest. My two married daughters were both at dinner and shouted in chorus, "Leave us out!" I felt near tears (from several drinks) and unfairly treated. I asked, "You don't trust my taste?" to which I received a resounding "No."

I decided to continue the memoir in the form of a novella. At this late date I couldn't bear to lapse into any delusions of reality in nonfiction.

Chapter 1

He went in a door and out another one ten feet away. It had been an old railroad flat he had remodeled, tearing down walls and painting. He liked the two doors close together. It gave him a sense of choice otherwise missing in his aging life.

Others who had remodeled railroad flats had stupidly closed off the extra door pretending it had never existed. He drove his neighbor in a prim bungalow quite crazy when he had a whim and circled in and out of his two doors. The neighbor was a retired academic, a delightfully bright codger who loved to speak vulgarly after a lifetime of propriety. The neighbor would open a fine wine he could afford on his generous retirement and wave him over to share it. He always went, even after he joined AA to preserve his marriage. He found out that fine wine encouraged a taste for fine wine and never precipitated a binge. If you drank half a bottle of Ducru-Beaucaillou you wanted more of it and nothing else, certainly not the rawness of whiskey or bilious beer.

He was what they called an "award winning poet," at least that was what his publisher called him on book jackets, though in fact he had never heard of any of the awards before he received them. So much for the immortality of poetry. He had even looked up the Pulitzer in the *World Almanac* at a doctor's office and been quite startled to see how many twentieth-century names had been forgotten. Meanwhile over a good Bordeaux his academic geezer neighbor would say, "Ontogeny recapitulates phylogeny" as if it were an obesity joke over which he chortled deeply. He himself could remember saying it in a coffee house before he flunked out of graduate school. His failure was due to "arrogance," the department chairman said. Young poets, even before they wrote a poem, tended to be prideful rather than properly self-effacing graduate students. Anyway, the department managed to grant him his master's after he published his first book of poems with an honored New York publisher. No one from the department had ever done that before. They were proud of him but not to the point where they would allow him to enroll in their Ph.D. program. Years more of him strutting the halls was an idea none of these fustian gentlemen could bear.

He and his wife weren't divorced but she lived a dozen miles out in the country outside Livingston, Montana, on a small farm with a big house. It had been her idea to get a house in town for becoming older and she was tired of taking care of such a large farmhouse of 3,800 square feet. He had also slipped on drinking which he had been able to manage in his early sixties.

He would take a chance and drive out at least twice a week and play with the dogs, often a disappointing experience because it had been quite warm and he would get there and be met wildly by the dogs but after a few minutes of play they'd settle back to sleeping on the thick grass of the lawn. He wanted them to play like they did as pups. The fact of the matter was that they were no longer pups. At ten they were about the same age in dog years as his own seventy. He slept in his studio when he came out to the farm, in a small cabin where he did his writing on the property near the big house. It wasn't elegant but simply workable.

He was taking a chance driving because he no longer had a driver's license. He had thought many times that the end of his rational marriage had come when they took his driver's license away. He was furious because it had been a mistake. He had stupidly admitted to the state cop that he had recently had spinal surgery. The cop asked if he was on narcotic pain medication and he clearly said, "No," but wasn't believed. As a matter of fact the first weeks after his surgery he had taken OxyContin but stopped despite the pain in his spine because the drug made his writing slurred and goofy. He couldn't write that way, not even in his journal which was frequently goofy all by itself.

He had also suffered from shingles for nearly three years though when the big sores subsided it was called postherpetic neuralgia. Whatever it was called it was plainly a double whammy about which nothing could be done medically. He had learned that doctors ignored shingles as an unprofitable disease until they had it themselves. There were no big fund-raisers for shingles. At the Department of Motor

Vehicles office he gave a bravura performance and they kept his license when he handed it over. "Give it back," he yelled.

Anyway, he had sent the governor an imprudent letter saying that he had written *Legends of the Fall,* his best-known book, and he needed to drive and explore new places in order to write and make a living. He couldn't very well sit home and write "Legends of the Yard." The letter didn't do any good although eventually he proved himself deserving and was able to drive again.

He had expected the trail into aging to be uneventful. On the contrary, who had ever heard of a white, Christian gentleman like himself losing his driver's license and sitting under a pine tree rather than driving to a friendly bar in town? Which of course is what he didn't need, a bar with old friends. He hated to think of the time and energy he had spent in a long life thinking about quitting smoking and drinking for the obvious health reasons. He had intermittently, briefly of course, been a health nut in his life. Once when they still lived in Michigan he lost twenty-five pounds in two months by walking four hours every morning, stopping for a rare cigarette, counting birds he liked, walking places in the Upper Peninsula where he had never walked before. The unknown always beckons. Early settlers always wondered what was over the next hill other than other hills. The vaunted reputation of Daniel Boone came from how thoroughly he had covered the landscape. He saved a village of starving people by going out and shooting a combination of ten deer and bears in one day, enough to feed everyone for a week.

When he was growing up in Michigan, his own father had been a good woodsman and had instructed him well.

When you think you're lost just sit and calm down. When you're frantic you lose your energy. Notice how the trees tend to lean a bit to the southeast. That's because of the pre-vailing winds and the immense storms from the northwest off Lake Superior. The day the freighter *Edmund Fitzgerald* went down it had blown over ninety miles per hour for a couple of days. He had been at his remote cabin then and did not stray from the protection of its sturdy logs. He read and listened to trees crashing down in the landscape. "Widow makers," they were called. He finally left the cabin for a much needed drink at the tavern. He drove down to the lakefront and watched as giant waves smothered the pier. Even in his car he shuddered in fear. The waves actually thundered.

By far the biggest jolt of aging was the disappearance, coming up on seventy, of his sexuality. The doctor improp-erly joked when he explained the problem. He was angry and the doctor said that it happens to everyone. In fact there was a bench in front of the town hall on which the same five old men sat every day called "the dead pecker bench." There were medications available now, and there was a joke at the tavern that if you had an erection more than three hours just visit the Starlite Alleys on women's bowling night and announce your problem. You'll get plenty of exercise. But the idea of taking a pill to get a hard-on left a bad taste.

He couldn't help trying it once the year before at the Modern Language Association annual meeting in Washing-ton, D.C., a city he loathed for political reasons but toler-ated when it was full of old writer friends. The target was a graduate student girl he had made love to years before when she was a sophomore. The price was that he had to write her a glowing recommendation to the Hunter College writing program in New York City. He readily agreed. She was a bit dumpy but used to have a nice body. They went to his room at the Mayflower after dinner and drank. She was in a hurry because she had to see an old boyfriend, also a writing professor. Unfortunately, the pill gave his gray room a deep green aura which irked him and then he came off in a minute. He apologized and then she quickly left to visit her friend without working up a sweat. To his surprise he noticed while watching CNN that he still had a hard-on, evidently a peculiarity of the pill. He went out in the street on the odds he might meet an acceptable pro, which he did a few blocks from the White House. They strolled along chatting amicably about music, which raised a warning flag in his head. A doctor friend had warned him never to sleep with a prostitute who also hung out with musicians as there was a higher incidence of AIDS in such women. Once again he apologized, gave her twenty bucks for the chat, and turned back to the hotel and the torpor of a thousand English professors at their evening meetings through which many dozed.

Years before when he was teaching at a university he had helped out the chairman who had hired him to do preliminary interviews with a half dozen creative writers applying for the vacancy. He had already tossed out about fifty résumés. The university was only a couple of hours from New York, a magic city, at least for writers. It was all in all very unpleasant, especially the air of pleading in their eyes, and interviewing the half dozen candidates was grueling.

The most obnoxious and smug man, also the best dressed with probably a rich wife, had gone so far as to write a good review of his own first book of poems and presumed that it gave him an inside track. He could barely wait to get him out of the room and pretended to make a phone call saying, "I'll be there in ten minutes," though ten minutes was far too long. He ended up giving the highest recommendation to the writer with the most kids.

The whole economics of work depressed him. He made a good salary, doubtless more than he deserved, but the candidate with the most children admitted that the night before he had missed the last bus back to the area of Virginia where he was staying with a relative. He had mostly walked the streets until about 4:00 a.m. and then went back to the hotel and took the elevator to the fifth floor where he recalled that there was a sofa near the elevator entrance. He had barely gotten to sleep when a bellhop woke him and offered to help him to his room. He deftly said that his roommate was sleeping with a very noisy woman. The bellhop laughed and continued on his way. He was then awakened at 7:00 a.m. by the first room service cart.

The award-winning poet asked the man why his college wouldn't pay for a room. He said it was because he had taken this last year off to write a comic novel. His wife and two daughters had all worked at McDonald's and they made it through okay. But he was not tenured and the department was replacing him with a young hotshot from Iowa. "That's why I'm here. I haven't sold the novel yet." It turned out the candidate had been cutting Christmas trees for four bucks an hour which was admittedly "chilly" in Michigan. He told

the man to go into the bedroom of his suite and gave him a
shooter, a two-ounce bottle of Canadian whiskey. He had
one himself and the man wobbled off to sleep.

It was a good story, he thought. They hired the man,
whose novel was published and did well. He wanted to quit
his new job and just write but his wife was fearful and told
him she would shoot him if she ever had to go back to work
at McDonald's. The family was overwhelmingly pleasant.
The award-winning poet reminded himself to keep his hands
off the man's two pretty teenage daughters.

He could date the moment desire had fled or when he
had truly noticed it. It was a late August afternoon in 2013.
It was warm and he sat at a table in the tavern. He was
alone because he always arrived at 4:00 p.m. and his friends
showed up at the more proper time of 5:00. There were two
girls at the bar and one of them was in a very short summer
skirt twirling on her bar stool. It was electrifying or would
have been in the past. He felt nothing and pinched himself
lightly to make sure he was actually alive. No, a curtain
had dropped and he wondered if it was a recent bad cold.
He certainly didn't feel the iron bite of lust which should
have been automatic. Not very far in the past, minutes to
be exact, he would have been up at the bar buying the girls
drinks, cajoling, letting drop a few credentials like "I was
just in New York seeing my publisher," looking down at the
smooth legs of the twirler and imagining her resplendent
pubis on his not so lonely pillow. Her friends came in and
the girls left but not before the twirler winked at him. The
display had been for his own frozen body. He couldn't even

manage to return the wink because his heart had abruptly darkened.

He had been distressed a long time by this nominal experience which wasn't nominal to him. It was more like a resounding crack of doom. So much of his life since youth had been consumed thinking about women.

One late afternoon when he and his neighbor John had sipped two bottles of good wine rather than one he had impulsively confessed that sex had "fled" his life.

"*Sic semper tyrannis,*" the man said.

"I forgot what that means."

"It means your tyrant is dead. Sex is the most powerful bully in our lives. Last year I saw an extraordinary number of young women going in and coming out of your place. They rarely lasted more than an hour. It all was an amusing diversion while I was cooking dinner. I certainly questioned your timing."

"I had to get at those before I got drunk which would render me unworkable. The minute they left I was free to have a big drink of whiskey or whatever."

"I assumed you were feeding them also."

"Not so, except some good cheese and Spanish olives I get Fed Exed from New York. It's my only food habit."

"You might not have figured out that I'm gay though I have a daughter from an early unfortunate marriage I made to please my parents. They had figured out that I was gay so I married to show them otherwise. You met my daughter two years ago."

"Yes, a lovely woman."

"It was mannerly of you not to make a run at her."

"When you had gone inside and I said something flirtatious to her she said she preferred boys from the car wash to academic men."

He had made a great deal when his novellas sold to Warner Bros. He wanted to quit teaching but his wife wanted him to hold on. She had her own money but was a maniac on the subject of saving for retirement. He had noted that she got this from her father who had saved a fair amount but then promptly died within a year of retiring. Her mother also had her own money but with the death of her husband she speedily went off to live in a nunnery for older women in Kentucky, an escape she had long planned. Since retirement was at least twenty years away he could not quite imagine that condition.

A dour confusion took hold of him. It slowly became apparent that it was caused by the quadri-schizoid nature of writing his own poems and novels, teaching, and now writing screenplays for what to him was lots of money. Starting out he received, he learned, the minimum fee of $50,000, which exceeded his academic salary for the entire year. Early the next year his agent got him $150,000 for a screenplay that was needed right away. He wrote it in three weeks. They said they "loved" it but never made the movie. Contrary to what he expected success had made him angry and unhappy. The reasons were elusive except that he had been thoroughly out of balance. He loaned a lot of money to friends and never got paid back except a thousand dollars apiece from two Native

American couples who lived near his cabin and needed to pay off trapping fines. Both couples visited in the following years with their debt contained in a cigar box and counted it out slowly. He didn't learn anything from being stiffed but kept stupidly waiting for people to repay. It occurred to him that times had changed. His father had taught him that a personal loan was like a gambling debt, a first priority.

The first signs of his wife wanting them to separate into different residences were at a time when he was drinking a great deal. Her point was well taken. He was no longer the man she had married who was calm, intelligent, mannerly, and slender. She used to love his body but his total weight gain since their marriage was seventy pounds. In his periods of walking mania he'd sometimes drop twenty-five pounds, and one year by dint of pure will he knocked off forty but wrote poorly. His very best work had come during a period when he was utterly indulgent at the table. How could he write well if he was thinking about food all the time? It didn't work to try to write about sex, doom, death, time, and the cosmos when you were thinking about a massive plate of spaghetti and meatballs. Of course all the extra weight had a bad effect on their sex life. He was too heavy for the orthodox missionary position plus his breath was bad from his gorging. She could only make love to him with her back turned. Also he was chronically fatigued. There was little left of him after a full day of writing. All that he wanted at the completion of the workday was a big drink, at least a triple. The tavern named a drink after him which was a quintuple tequila with a dash of Rose's lime juice. He quit drinking it when the price of his favorite tequila, Herradura, skyrocketed due to an agave disease in Mexico and the fact that fine tequila had become fashionable in Japan. He could afford it but resented it like the poor boy he once was. He had become a free spender with his habitual table always full with friends and acquaintances, some of the latter hanging in there for free drinks.

In a peacemaking ceremony with his wife he agreed to have no more hard liquor in the home, just wine. He played it honest for about a month, then began to feel like a deprived artist. When he shopped for wine at the liquor store he would buy a half dozen shooters. He continued buying and hiding them, mostly in his studio, until he had fifty. Such were his alcohol needs that he made a clumsy map of the hiding places knowing his own forgetfulness. Now that he had devised this stupid rule to please his wife he could sneak a shooter with the glass of red wine he had late in the afternoon. To his credit he never drank while writing except for a sip as he drew his work to a close for the day. He and a friend had a game while they were reading Faulkner, finding passages where it was easy to see that the great man was deep in the bag. Faulkner would fall off his horse and then get drunk to alleviate the pain. Anything could make him go on a comatose bender, even getting the Nobel Prize. A horrid photo of his face after shock treatment was fortunately blocked from publication, though it later surfaced. Seeing it actually made the award-winning poet think about quitting drinking, a very rare and insincere impulse. His own father drank sparingly, not much beyond a cold beer when he was grilling on a hot summer day. He explained that when you had five children and a small salary it was one of the things you cut out. He himself tended to overdrink both when he was broke and when he had extra money. One excuse was that drinking too much guaranteed marital fidelity. He had never told his wife this because he didn't want to be closely observed during sober periods, but it is a well-known fact among drinkers that too much and you won't get the necessary hard-on. He never met anyone accessible anyway except the tavern tarts. He had tried one the year before but she puked within a minute of entering the motel and the smell made his tender organ instantly wilt. She rinsed her face and then finally said, "What's wrong with you?" He was too well mannered to say that the smell of vomit turned him off.

Students were strictly off-limits these days, in no small part due to feminism, but in the old days when he was teaching everything was possible and ignored by all. He clearly recalled some domestic horror caused by professors and their student lovers. Once he had taken a lovely girl on a ride to a big woodlot outside of town not knowing that his wife was following with his pistol at a distance in her car. She had become suspicious when she found a note in his jacket that said, "I just love it when you go down on me."

His wife crept cautiously down the log trail and through the woods. She knew the area well from bird-watching. She had seen many spring warblers in the carapace of hardwood trees, also morel mushrooms to pick whose season was the same time as the warblers arrived from the south.

She was now close enough to hear the sound of their coupling and the habitual overloud shout of her husband's orgasm. She pulled the .38-caliber pistol from her shoulder holster and fired the pistol near the open window of their car. It was immensely loud.

"I'm shot. I'm dead," he yelled, dramatically.

The girl bailed out the far side of the car and sprinted down the log road deeper into the woods. She was nude from the waist down which would be a problem with mosquitoes. She ran amazingly fast and another shot was fired in the air to encourage her and perhaps discourage fucking another married man. His wife leveled the pistol at him who had recovered enough to swig from a pint of Canadian whiskey.

"I can legally shoot you," she said.

"Tell someone who gives a shit," he replied jauntily with whiskey courage.

She tilted the gun and shot out the far window. He cringed and yelled "No" beginning to sob. She looked down at his guilty peter thinking of shooting him there but it had retreated like a turtle's head. She threw the pistol into the woods after he said, "Don't kill me before I finish the screenplay or you'll be out a hundred grand," his whisper choking him.

She walked back to her car feeling rather light-headed after performing a comic marital scene. "Finishing a screenplay" became a family joke whenever she wanted to torment him or truncate one of his prepared marital speeches.

Later on when he thought about this event his heart gave an extra thump and he felt lucky that he hadn't shit his pants. A few days later, after his class on the modern novel, the girl said that her ass was covered with mosquito bites. This turned him on and he wanted to see the bites but she said, "Nothing doing. I better get an A or I'm telling your chairman that you're a sexual deviant." She knew her power and didn't bother writing a term paper. She merely doodled on her finals. He couldn't blame her, wondering how she had made it home half nude. Later he found the pistol with difficulty in the woods. It was a keepsake to him. It had been his father's and grandfather's, an old-fashioned Colt revolver. The story was that his grandfather had shot at a neighbor he suspected of setting fire to his barn. The neighbor moved away with a hole in his leg which ended the argument.

He grew quite tired of the early beliefs that he felt were forced upon him. His mother had pounded into him certain children's books of a semireligious nature. One of them maintained that above all he must be "strong, brave, and true." To his usual questioning his mother was hasty in her explanations. To her all of his questions had become maddening because she frequently could see that he didn't believe her answers. "How do birds fly?" was a killer that she left to her husband. They went to the town library and checked out many helpful texts. He recalled from walking in the woods that when you picked up a dead bird it was startling how light it was, even a comparatively large crow. Strong, brave, and true wasn't so hard except for "true" which remained something of a mystery. "Strong" had always been the easiest because at his father's insistence even as a boy he exercised relentlessly so as not to become "puny," an ugly word his father used. He also worked and would weed gardens and mow lawns for fifteen cents an hour. He disliked washing cars so he charged a full quarter for that.

He became by far the strongest boy in his class at school and well into his forties he could beat the workingmen at arm wrestling contests at the tavern.

Of course he knew that strength of this sort was quite irrelevant in today's world. Nothing beyond the ability to depress a computer key was wanted, except if you worked in construction or needed a cement block layer which he had been after he flunked out of graduate school. They lived a threadbare existence because back then out of pride he had refused to let his wife take any money from her well-off parents. It was utterly brutal work, especially in cold weather. You added a little salt to the mortar if it was below freezing though this was illegal or dishonorable as it weakened the bind between blocks. Once he was shivering so hard holding up an eighty-five-pound corner block that he dropped it, crushing several toes. At emergency they had to cut off his heavy Red Wing boot. During his recuperation, brief because they were broke, he made the understandable decision to return to graduate school to get a master's degree. The department was pleased to accept him back because he had published a first book of poems with W. W. Norton and a novel with Simon and Schuster. Later on he frequently regretted what a heartless prick he had been. Success didn't help that much because it couldn't wipe away the years of bad behavior. In one shabby rental house he kept the thermostat at fifty-five degrees because they couldn't afford much fuel. Why suffer from cold due to pride?

Their first child Robert died almost immediately from a bad heart. They had two daughters, one ten years after the other, who were the joy in their life. But when they married and left home he was saddened thinking, "What now?" There was always alcohol. What saved his sorry neck was buying a fairly remote cabin in Michigan's Upper Peninsula as a place to escape to. Typical of him, he didn't even go inside the cabin before he bought it. Since he obviously didn't care for the human race to speak of he kept happy with the profusion of birds and the more than occasional bear that entered the yard to rob the bird feeder. A bear would take a big mouthful of sunflower seeds then become ruminative as he chewed. He got to know one old male so well that when he came home from the tavern late at night quite polluted he'd stop on his two-track driveway, the bear would approach and put his chin on the windowsill, and he'd scratch his ears. This was admittedly stupid and when he learned more about bears from his friend Mike he stopped doing it. He'd leave out any surplus of fish on a stump at least a hundred yards from the cabin. Finally, the old male no longer visited and he deduced that it had died of old age or had been shot by the oversupply of bear hunters who visited the area each fall with their hounds.

Both of their daughters moved to Montana and after a few years of loneliness and longish late-summer trips he and his wife gave up on the beauties of ever more crowded northern Michigan, sold the farm, and moved to Montana. It was harder for his wife than for him. She made all of the moving arrangements and could only find an unpleasant rental to stay in for the few weeks of searching for a house. She found a big farmhouse on about thirty acres and she made extensive remodeling plans with carpenters and then returned to their little casita near the Mexican border for the fall, winter, and cold rainy early spring.

Eventually despite his wife's caution he was sprung forever from teaching by screenwriting which gradually became its own hell because out of pure greed he took on too much work. He couldn't quite believe he was making so much money but there was absolutely no positive emotional quotient to the money. It largely depressed him. A morning phone call from Hollywood could ruin a day's work. During these years in Montana he fished constantly, a boyhood obsession, but occasionally missed the morbid routine of teaching. Years before he had been hired at Stony Brook out on Long Island through the graces of an ex-professor who had become powerful. The work was very easy. He taught only one course and also assisted the chairman. He had a corner office into which he moved an easy chair. No straight back chairs were in the office. The easy chair was awkward for the countless professors who came in to complain about the injustices of teaching. The chairman allowed him to decide who taught what and he was widely disliked for his arrogance. He taught one very popular course in twentieth-century poetics, which was the real reason for the easy chair. At the time miniskirts were obligatory and attractive girls from his class would come in and plop in the deep chair. The visuals were wonderful.

With his students he was sometimes coarse and abusive when they asked him for writing advice. He had been hired to teach recent American literature not creative writing. He had gotten off on the wrong foot with his colleagues over and over by maintaining Gabriel García Márquez was an American writer in the larger sense. Both north and south of the United States were the "Americas" including Canada.

Objections surrounded him but he didn't care because his work was doing very well. It was up to Margaret Atwood if she wanted to be American or Canadian not the English professors of the world.

He would act in the manner of Leo Tolstoy who, when Rilke told him he must write, said, "Then write for God's sake." Even nastier was Faulkner who in answer to the question of what a writer needs said, "Paper and pencil." In other words, figure it out for yourself, there are no shortcuts. You have to give your entire life to it.

He looked forward to his seventieth birthday and it finally arrived as it must. On this birthday he planned on becoming a free-floating geezer, above criticism from both others and himself. He drank when he chose and after a couple of notorious sexual failures he was deterred and stopped trying. He finally asked a doctor friend who told him that the nine pills he took daily since his spinal surgery would kill sex for an elephant or a whale. He thought of discarding his pills but then he didn't want to die quite yet. As a beginning writer he had planned on publishing books until the moment of death, hopefully twenty of them at least, a nineteenth-century program but as a young writer he fashioned himself a nineteenth-century man, vigorous, athletic, hardworking, bold. Unfortunately he was ten books behind schedule. In recent months he had completed both a novel and a book of novellas but now at seventy he was utterly exhausted. Once again he consulted his doctor drinking friend who diagnosed complete exhaustion and that he had blown out his adrenals. Since he didn't know what adrenals were and wasn't curious he settled for the fact that they were blown out. He quit work of any sort except for an occasional poem and the journal he kept and took to sleeping a great deal of the day plus the night. The shingles and neuralgia left him without REM sleep at night because his salves and pills didn't last for long, but in the day he could apply a lot of salve and nap for an hour in comfort. He recovered from the overexertion of writing two books at once but the exhaustion would never completely go away.

At the bar since his seventieth birthday his friends had taken to calling him "old man." This amused rather than troubled him. Most were in their fifties. A couple in their twenties were permitted at the hallowed table because he judged them to be good writers. Three of the men at the table were old friends, and artists, who were always more vivid than writers. They also cooked much better than poets and novelists, he had no idea why. He was the putative master of ceremonies of the table and had the errant talent of keeping the conversation going whenever everyone flagged. Occasionally Dolly, a poet, would join them. She was brave enough to withstand the vulgarity of their dialogue and answer them in kind, sometimes going over the edge and embarrassing them. It was comic to him that several of his friends refused to acknowledge the advent of aging. Maybe subconsciously they realized it because they often acted afflicted with a false heartiness, telling stories of totally fictional seductions without realizing that no one believed them. He thought long and hard about male vanity and the need to prolong these manly delusions past the point of any possible credibility, similar to wanting to go to war until you actually got there. He remembered the old quote he had read somewhere, "There is no God but reality. To seek him elsewhere is the action of the fall." What was the point in pretending you were any age but the one you were?

One hot afternoon at the tavern he dropped a modest bomb he had written in his journal. "We all are on death row living in cells of our own devising." This started a loud quarrel between the two who took full responsibility for what they were and the four others who blamed a panoply of circumstances. His own father had liked to say, "Why blame anybody else because you're a fuckup?" He favored this one, admitting that everything that had gone radically wrong in his life could be traced to causes that sat in his own lap. He had also been taught that it was *unmanly* to be forever blaming someone else for one's problems. Dolly, the poet, piped up to say she had been painfully raped by three boys when she was eleven. There was dead silence, until a stupid drunk said, "The exception proves the rule," and he was roundly booed. Everyone else apologized to Dolly for this horrible thing. He had always thought this "exception" statement to be obtuse.

Of late his spirits had taken an upturn from his habitually dour attitude toward life. He continued to use his studio despite separating from his wife, and one afternoon he was in there listening to Schubert on NPR when a house wren appeared at the screened window and began aggressively singing back at the radio. This went on for quite a while and he recalled from his boyhood as a nature obsessive that a marsh wren has a more involved language than a house wren. He was troubled he could come up with no further memory about wrens. This one nested in a blocked stovepipe

on the roof and perhaps thought that the Schubert was a
competitive bird, although it then seemed to be excitedly
singing along with the Schubert bird. He tried to recall
something from the Internet his wife had passed along, how
at the University of Chicago researchers were scientifically
monitoring the dream life of finches. They found that finches
have dream songs they never sing otherwise. Just like us, he
thought. The gifts of childhood were the trees, rivers, birds,
flowers. He wondered where his little guidebooks from that
era were. He went down in the studio basement looking for
old stray book boxes. He found the field guide to trees, not
his favorite. He recalled asking in Sunday school why God
was so messy in creating so many kinds of trees. The teacher
became angry at him for questioning God. He cried on the
long walk home feeling like a sure-thing sinner though deep
within himself he couldn't stop questioning the immense
variety of species on earth. It was confusing for a boy.

The night before he had experienced a repeat of the
most disconcerting nightmare of his life. Sometimes when
he had it he awoke vomiting on the floor, bending out of bed
and letting go. It had all started soon after he lost his left
eye in an accident. A girl, a playmate, had shoved a broken
beaker into his eye that she'd picked up from the trash pile
at the edge of the woods behind the hospital. He walked
next door to the doctor's wife Mrs. Kilmer's and she cleaned
him up and called her husband and his parents. He ended
up in a hospital down in Grand Rapids for a month. When
he got home finally, the left side of his face was covered with
bandages. The doctor had saved the life of his eye but not his
vision. About a week later the flu swept through the town

of Reed City and he got a severe case. Another week later
the annual town minstrel show was scheduled. No one in
town ever missed it but a few drunks and a smattering of the
very poor like the dump picker, his wife, and their daughter
for whom they took up a class collection every year to buy
her socks for the winter or she'd go without. He lied to his
parents and said he was feeling better when in fact he was
still nauseous and shivering with fever. They couldn't find a
sitter and his parents very much wanted to see the minstrel
show. They wrapped him in his father's deer hunting coat to
protect him from the cold November evening and the small
auditorium which was always too cool. They sat down in
the front row and the show made them dizzy, and a fat man
sitting next to them kept farting. Ordinarily, he would have
found this funny but in his current condition it amplified his
living nightmare. He was deeply embarrassed. All the people
onstage were in blackface, including a chorus of women who
also danced. The men were recognizable as town leaders despite their heavy makeup. Everyone sang very loudly and
poorly, he thought. No one for sure was a Bing Crosby. He
dozed for a few minutes and when he looked out again he was
sweating with fever and the stage was whirling as if time were
passing in an old movie. He vomited in his father's hunting
coat and partly on the floor. It was very loud and the stage
action paused. "We've had a reaction to our performance,"
a minstrel yelled and everyone laughed. His father whisked
him out with his mother in tow. It was early November and
there was some fresh fallen powdery snow. When his father
put him down near the car he took a handful of the snow and
wiped it across his face and mouth. It felt delicious.

"We never should have taken him to that piece of shit," his father said angrily.

"I agree," said his mother.

"We're sorry son," they said in unison.

When they got home he sat down at the kitchen table with his mother and weakly tried to help her clean the coat with kitchen washcloths and a brush. Instead he fell off his chair and knocked himself out. His father carried him to his bedroom and tucked him in. He vomited again and then slept, not awakening until the following morning.

This experience shaped itself into a nightmare that followed him the rest of his life. It disheartened him to the point that in his forties he went to a mind doctor. That helped for a year or so but then he was revisited. He never again was able to attend a stage performance of any kind. Eventually he also had to opt out of the habitual routine for poets, that of reading their poems out loud before an audience. Either the day before or late the night of the reading he would be revisited by the nightmare until the night whirled around him. And the feeling of nausea would return, certainly one of the most unpleasant feelings of the human animal. So he was high and dry, shorn of the renown, if not fame and extra money. He wasn't really able to entertain an audience and had little interest in trying. The minstrel ogre would arise before a reading and he imagined that he had smeared himself in blackface.

It was darkly comic to think of one's life as haunted by minstrels. They were ultimately fake humans, derisive not to speak of dishonest. And nearly all poets were liars in his opinion too. They couldn't possibly be the men they were reading about with the usual catalog of fine qualities. After attending and giving at least a hundred poetry readings he could remember only one that struck him as a hundred percent genuine and honest. A poet named, simply enough, Red Pine read from an ancient Chinese poet he had translated, called Stonehouse. Red Pine read with quiet integrity just what he'd translated. Usually after a reading he was in a private snit and needed a drink, but now he walked down and looked at the harbor, his spine still tingling. The other true exception was Gary Snyder. He never wanted Snyder's readings to end.

Early in the spring he took a ride thirty miles or so into the country, a weekly pilgrimage. In a village there was a small corner restaurant operated by a large old lady. She slow cooked a very large chunk of meat, at least a dozen pounds, all night long. It was the best ever in his memory. He had come late once at noon and gone without so he tried to get there at ten-thirty before the main rush. She served it as a hot roast beef sandwich with a scoop of mashed potatoes, homemade bread and a marvelous gravy, and a side of her own peppery corn relish. This dish is everywhere served at diners and truck stops as the way to get the most for your money, truly filled up. He had eaten the dish a lot as a woebegone young beatnik hitchhiking senselessly back and forth between San Francisco and New York City.

The ride over that day had been fine and warm with the first tinges of pastel green in the pastures. Even the cows looked happy, optimistic now that another wretched winter had passed. The old woman, Edna by name, started serving at 10:30 a.m. because many of her farmer customers had had their breakfasts at 5:00 a.m. before feeding and milking chores. Edna said, "I don't sleep good since Frank died." Frank, her husband, was known for raising good beef cattle and had died the year before from a heart attack while branding.

The poet pulled in early beside a single pickup and had time for a final cigarette before entering. Through his open passenger-side window he smelled something bad and heard scuffling. Within the caged back of the pickup there was a massive Hampshire sow. He was startled because the sow looked just like Old Dolly, his grandfather's prime sow, but that was over fifty years ago and pigs rarely live beyond twelve years, so it couldn't be her. Besides, if he remembered right, she was butchered when she went dry, her meat frozen and given to a social worker to distribute to the poor.

He went inside and said hello to the only occupant, an old farmer with trembling hands.

"Fine sow you got out there. A Hampshire I think?"

"Mostly Hampshire. Something else I haven't figured out. The man I bought her from as a piglet years ago was moving back east. Maybe Duroc."

"We had one that looked just like her way back when."

"Good time to get back in the business if you grow corn. Pork is high. Hard to grow corn in Montana. Lucky for me my younger brother grows good corn over near Billings. She's for sale."

"How much?" He felt inspired. Why not?

"Three hundred bucks. Cash on the barrelhead. I'm retiring, selling out after sixty years of farming. Moving to town right here. We live too far in the country for my wife. In a weak moment I promised to take her to Hawaii when I retired. The sow's going to farrow in two weeks. You can make your money back on her farrow. She's always had at least ten piglets."

"Sold," he said and drew this man, Fred by name, a map to get to his place. "Give me three days. I've got to build a pen." He counted out three C-notes from the secret corner in his wallet for emergencies. It was never safe enough from his wife and two daughters, both long gone and married to hardworking young men in this troubled economy.

On the way home he kept thinking it's now or never and how he would tell his wife.

She had three horses, two of which didn't like him one bit, and a pasture of ten acres with a white board fence. They had first boarded horses in a small stable with fencing they built themselves in the young, salad days of their marriage when they had bought a little farm for nineteen grand. Nothing cost that much those days, even a car. Now she had her own horses.

He stopped for a drink at a roadhouse. He only wanted one for courage but had a double and a beer chaser to make sure it worked. After all he didn't need to tell her right away. Luckily he had enough lumber from an old chicken coop he had torn down when they moved in. In the beginning they had chickens for a couple of years but found them too irritating. Over the years, though, he had wanted pigs, especially when he was a little depressed over his mediocre writing career. During the truly melancholy period of his childhood after he lost his left eye he would sit outside his grandpa's pigpen on a piece of stump and watch the creatures. Once after the sow had farrowed ten piglets Grandpa had moved her into an adjoining pen and let him sit in the pen with the piglets, in a dry corner away from the muck and shit. It was pure joy for his bewildered spirit. The piglets swarmed over him and loved having their ears and tummies scratched. He especially liked the little runt of the litter and on his request he was given the runt for his special care. He named her Shirley after a girl he liked in the second grade.

He was still in his pig trance when he stopped at a farm equipment and feed store. He cautioned himself to remain alert to signs of his bipolar problem without admitting to himself it was manic to buy a five-hundred-pound sow over lunch. He made a note on his car tablet to buy six cedar fence posts, a trough for eating, and a tank for water. He would build the pen against the wall and around the back door of his studio. He remembered to buy five bushels of feed, recalling that a healthy sow would eat a ton of feed in a year. He could hear the cash register singing when it occurred to him if she farrowed eight or ten or whatever he would also be feeding them after she weaned them. His dad had told him that after mating a sow would give birth in three months, three weeks, and three days or a total of 116 days. It was all so scientific. Or so he thought being largely ignorant of science except astronomy.

He didn't write for two and a half days because he was thinking fondly of pigs. Not a word. His old friend

Cyrus Pentwater had quit both writing and drinking when he began raising both llamas and ostriches. He had read that raising ostriches had turned into a scam of sorts. You paid thirty grand for a breeding pair and the only way of getting your money back was to breed more breeding pairs and sell them to someone eager and thick skulled. They said the meat was good and tasted like beef. Then why not buy beef which was considerably cheaper? And who could butcher an ostrich that had been somewhat of a pet for years? In the tavern where men talk about many things they know nothing about, there was a rumor that ostriches had kicked several owners to death. Some checked their computers and could find no proof but they all wanted to believe it like stories of vipers that could kill you in five seconds.

The first evening he was singing a little song of pig breed names from all over the world while watching CNN about the horrors of Syria. His kind neighbor next to the railroad flat had brought up a list on his computer. "Hampshire, Arapawa Island, Mukota, Lacombe, Mulefoot, Iberian, Chester White, Dutch Landrace, Guinea Hog, Swabian-Hall swine." He didn't see his wife right behind him. She tousled his hair.

"Your hair is getting thin with age."

"So I've noticed. Isn't yours?"

"I don't want to talk about it. What were those gibberish names you were singing?"

"The names of llama breeds," he said thinking quickly.

"I thought a llama was just a llama."

"No more than a horse is just a horse."

"What are you going to do with this llama?"

"They can carry your gear into the mountains."

"You never hiked into the mountains except in your fiction."

"I never had a llama to carry the gear."

"Your turn to do the dishes, baby doll." They dreaded chores now that they were semi-separated.

This llama thing was getting out of hand and he was setting himself up for a mudbath when his giant sow arrived.

He slept quite early that night after seeing a National Geographic special on hyenas. It made him want a hyena pet though he'd heard a hyena could bite off your arm clean as a whistle. A hyena doubtless would look at his pig like a fifty-course meal. Hemingway shot hyenas in the gut to make them suffer. He thought they were lesser creatures than the lordly lions which he also shot, presumably not in the gut. A friend had met a Masai in Kenya with one side of his body feathered by scar tissue got from spearing a lion at close quarters while it was charging, which entitled him to carry the heroic lion shield. His friend said that this was courageous compared with hunters who shot lions at two hundred yards.

He gave his wife a perfunctory kiss goodnight on the neck, a habit they had continued. On the way out the back door he noticed he had forgotten to wash the dishes and quickly did so. Fair is fair. One cooks a nice veal roast and the other washes the dishes.

He gingerly touched the blisters on his right hand from the rough-handled post hole digger. His hands were no longer trained for manual labor. His friendly butcher neighbor had come over early that morning. Zack, in his late thirties, would test a cedar post and say, "A little deeper, friend." It had been a cool morning but he dripped with sweat over the holes. Zack nailed the pen boards on the inside of the posts so that the heavy hog wouldn't pop the nails leaning on the boards. Thanks to Zack they rigged up the pen in an hour, then laid out the trough and water tank.

"You can't make no money on pigs without growing your own corn," Zack said.

"I know that. I'm looking for companionship."

"That's what dogs and wives are for," Zack laughed. He had a pit bull, Charley, that was less friendly than a scorpion.

He very much needed a drink though his skin prickled with thrills when he saw the finished pen with separate enclosures for the sow and her piglets. Zack had said you had to be careful that the sow didn't roll over and crush members of her own litter. Something else to worry about on questionable planet earth. When they first split up his wife had destroyed all vestiges of alcohol in the household including the studio. He had seen it coming and taped two airline shooters up under the lowest shelf of the bookshelf with ever-useful duct tape. Now he swallowed both of the little bottles without mixing them, coughed violently, and felt the warm glow rising. He felt like writing but his rule was never to write while drinking. He was a puritan about his work, never keeping food in the studio because food drew in flies and he didn't want to interrupt his work by trying to swat flies. He certainly wasn't this careful about anything else in life. His wife had visited while they worked and had commented that it was an awfully strong fence for a llama when a little wire would have sufficed.

"Maybe the llama will have babies," he said weakly. Maybe he was a fiction writer and poet because he couldn't stand to tell the simple truth.

"You better work on your fence, farmer boy," she replied.

The immediate ten acres was fenced but it was in modest disrepair. "I'll take care of it," Zack kindly said.

"You spoil him but then everyone does except me," she said and wandered back to the house with Zack watching her butt sway in her khaki shorts.

"She's a looker, that's for sure. If you're creating great art you don't have time to fence."

"That's right," he said. "We'll want sheep fence so the little piglets don't escape. I'll pay you fifteen bucks an hour to put up the fence." He felt dreamy at the idea of watching piglets roam around out the windows while he wrote. Maybe he could get a novel out of the idea of a poor artist raising pigs to support his art.

Early in the morning the day after they finished the pen he got a call from the farmer to say he was loading the pig. He asked for fifteen more minutes and fled his railroad flat with a cold cup of coffee from the night before, leaving behind a graduate student's wife in his bed. Her husband had been on a fishing trip. He had been trying the night before and had done poorly at love. He had hoped to make up for it this morning and had said so. She'd looked at him sleepily. "I got to take delivery of a pig out at my farm," he said.

When he got there the farmer was backed up to the pen and leading the pig down a double wide plank. He saw his wife who was watching. He parked and walked down the new path to the pen. His wife was helping the old farmer shove the heavy planks back into his pickup. She turned glaring at him.

"You asshole," she said simply.

"I thought my llama would need company," he said quickly.

"You're a natural born liar," she said.

The old farmer laughed. "I know someone else who wants her. You'll have to decide fast as you don't want to move her too close to her farrowing. She'll feed you all year. A llama can't do that."

He leaned over the pen and scratched her ear which pleased her. He deeply felt she was beautiful. This is called pride of ownership.

"I'm thinking of shooting her in the head," his wife said, and walked back to the house.

"Is she serious?" the farmer asked.

"I doubt it," he said and gave the pig two shovelfuls of the ground feed in the trough about which she was very happy.

"Call me if you need advice," the farmer said. They shook hands and the farmer left.

He went into his studio thinking he might write a few paragraphs on his new sow but he was far too excited. They had delivered him a supersized dog house, now a pig house, and he had spread out three bales of straw for her comfort. He gazed at her out the window while playing Mozart's Symphony No. 41, his last. He dozed with pleasure as the pig was dozing after lunch. He asked himself why he had waited so long to fulfill his childhood dream of owning his own pig.

He had always been irritated by Wordsworth's line about the child being father of the man. He didn't doubt its basic truth but it was the deterministic aspect that bothered him. Of late he had been perplexed by religious threads that entered his thinking, originating as they did from a devout period he went through between the ages of eleven and fifteen. Jesus had been his boyhood hero rather than Superman or any of the other comic book heroes his friends favored. A neighbor friend was obsessed with growing up to be Dick Tracy and having a wrist radio to communicate. This friend died in Vietnam and so far as he knew had never owned a cell phone. This all had come to a head when he was a senior in college in a philosophy seminar. He had brought up the idea that in youth it was easy to acquire beliefs that were difficult later to disbelieve. For instance he still believed in the Resurrection and felt eerie about it at Easter time. He was roundly derided except by the professor who thought it was an interesting question. There was a lot of condescension and ridicule and general raw spirits. A lit student pointed out that the French poet Guillaume Apollinaire had written that Jesus held the world's high altitude record. There was laughter and he recalled that at the minstrel show he had been enraged when those onstage sang what was then called a Negro spiritual in their mock black voices. This was clearly sacrilege as his minister would certainly have said. The professor interrupted to point out that what he had brought up was particularly true of young people with hateful beliefs such as antiblack racism or anti-Semitism that seemed to continue to follow them throughout their lives. He jumped in and agreed, then added in his own level of derision that those in the class only believed in beer, golf, and pussy. The professor chided him for vulgarity but with a slight smile of agreement.

Now all of these years later he was again burdened by those hidden beliefs. He could not tell you *why* he believed in the Resurrection but it had never occurred to him to disbelieve it. He took to saying little prayers well under his breath. His main problem was alcohol which was easy to acknowledge. He prayed and then didn't go to the bar for a whole week. He had his shooters at home but no full bottle. One evening he drank seven shooters but didn't get all that far. He felt he should have been drunker. Now his friends called, really just tavern friends, and asked if he was sick. "Yes, we all are," he said cryptically. He didn't necessarily mean alcoholism. He rarely exceeded two drinks a day, he told himself. It was the regularity of the tavern habit that had begun to drive him crazy.

And then there were his fears that something might happen to his piglets in his absence. The sow was safe from stray dogs — her enormous jaws would make mincemeat out of any hapless mutt. But the piglets were vulnerable. Now he could tend them after a long day's writing. To be frank the pigs were now far more interesting to him than his tavern friends.

As a child he had read a great deal including the forbidden so-called adult books. His father had saved his own youthful library that included travel adventure books by Richard Halliburton, all of Zane Grey, and a peculiar series about a young man named Tom Swift. His reading was aided by childhood illnesses like a severe case of pneumonia that

kept him in bed for a month of reading as did his severe
eye injury. He began to think of school as being quite boring compared with the pleasures of reading. *Tom Swift and
His Electric Rifle* had been far ahead of its time back in the
teens and twenties, and those books encouraged him to think
about the world in a more organized way and develop his
own theories. For instance, because he first got religion in
the summer, it occurred to him that God must have come
up from the ground and entered him through his bare feet.
Why not? His feet were bare all summer long and he thought
at times that he felt messages in his feet, his telephone to
the spirit world. At age nine he dropped this theory on his
Sunday school class and it was unpopular. Everyone else insisted that God was in the sky. The teacher was sympathetic
remembering the goofiness of her own conversion which
was when she was out in nature and the trees were speaking to her. He persisted in trying to figure out life, keeping
track in a diary, so it was not surprising when he became a
writer. Once when they were trout fishing he mentioned his
God in the ground theory to his father who responded that
he always thought God was a trout stream. Hearing this he
began to worry about Godless deserts with no rivers and
said so. His father replied that deserts were full of arroyos
and dry riverbeds, the rivers of the past, and God didn't
need active water present because he didn't drink water. He
brooded about his father's words for months and became
excited about the future and going west to sense God in dry
riverbeds. His father also advised that there was no money
in theology. This fell upon deaf ears as he never thought
much about money.

He got two dollars a week as an allowance, plus what he could earn mowing lawns, washing cars, weeding gardens. He saved as much as he could to follow the path of the great Halliburton when he got old enough. He wanted to criss-cross the world and have many perilous, but not too perilous, adventures. He would doubtless save a beautiful native girl from a giant anaconda, whacking off its head with his trusty machete. Just recently an awareness of women had entered his life strongly. The culture was looking for an extra four years for college which would needlessly delay adventure. The world gave one so many reasons to be pissed off at it. The age factor was a matter of great impatience. The young want time to hurry, the old usually want it to slow down.

He had found out he was bright completely by accident. A man from the university in a nearby city needed a guinea pig to take tests as part of a course. He got two bucks an hour, a real windfall, to take five different IQ tests and late in the process he had snooped through the man's papers when he went out to pee and noted his scores for the first four tests ranged from 163 to 171. He didn't know what this meant, if anything of consequence. Religion had loosened some screws in his head and at this point in life he didn't want to be brilliant, he just wanted to be ordinary.

At fourteen he didn't want to fear for his sanity. One of his few literate friends, albeit goofy, had lent him a volume of Gurdjieff and Ouspensky and he had carelessly experimented with "out of body" trances wherein he could do such things as visit other planets and walk on the ocean floor. He had chosen the Mindanao bays, the deepest part of the ocean, but hadn't imagined the bottom would be pitch black

other than for a few phosphorescent creatures. The problem
was that once he got there he couldn't get back in his body
back home. He had started in the evening and struggled
to return to normality most of the night. This frightened
him terribly and in the light of a summer dawn he was very
happy to recognize objects in his room, especially a print
of a Modigliani portrait and another of *The Birth of Venus*
by Sandro Botticelli. Evidently Venus was born full grown
and certainly the sexiest person in humankind. At his age
she gave him a frequent hard-on. Once liberated back to
the ordinary he vowed never again to errantly play with his
mind. The imagination was too large to play with.

He spent a few weeks of forlorn boredom in the very
early spring and then began running every day after school
at the suggestion of the coach who one day timed him while
his large boys' phys ed class ran the half mile. The coach was
cagey noting that he had won by a couple hundred yards and
his time was certainly good enough for the school track team.
By working out relentlessly he was able by May to take
second place by only a few seconds in the county championship meet. For a few years it was wonderful. However, he
stupidly ruined it all the following summer when he gained
thirty pounds of muscle on the advice of another coach. He
gained the weight to play football. At present he viewed this
as a lifelong mistake thinking that though the muscle was
pleasant it did him no good, and he could pointillistically
trace all of his various aches and pains in middle age back
to the injuries he had sustained in high school football. He
was a running guard on offense and a middle linebacker on
defense. In one game he was called and the team penalized

for unnecessary roughness. He was ashamed when later he learned he had needlessly injured a boy on a team from a neighboring town. At heart he was a secret Quaker and football was pure violence. The coach was always telling him to "hit them harder." The coach wanted him to put opposing players "out of commission." He kept it to himself but wondered what the point of the "game" was if your intention was to hurt people badly. His girlfriend was one of the cheerleaders and a bit dim-witted though lovely.

Track had been freedom but football just a dumb brutal game. He had felt one concussion for years afterward.

Chapter 2

He had begun calling the sow Darling or D, elongated to Dee in his midwestern drone which, earlier in life when the comedian was current, people said reminded them of Herb Shriner. This was meant as ridicule but he didn't mind because he liked Herb Shriner. Darling farrowed and gave him nine piglets. He watched it all leaning on the pen. He said to himself ironically, "The miracle of birth," but in truth he felt it deeply. It was a lot to ask of a female. Tragically the third day he lost his favorite, the runt of the litter he had called Alice. The sow had rolled over and crushed one of her children. He carried the little body into the studio and put her on the desk. He sobbed. He had intended her to be his best friend. They would take walks together every day and if she got tired he would carry her home like he had done with one of his dogs. He wrapped her carefully in a big red bandanna thinking that she was yet another of the deep injustices of life. He dug a hole near the pen and decorated it with a circle of rocks. He put her wrapped body down in the hole, dropped a handful of earth on it, and said an actual prayer for the deliverance of her soul. He had crisscrossed two yellow pencils in the shape of a cross, glued them together, and stuck them in Alice's grave.

He was pleased that he didn't separate his own life from that of Alice, or a crow or a dog. Over the years when one of his dogs died he thought that maybe he should go along for the ride, affection causing a sympathetic suicide. Of course he held back though Alice's death struck deep. What held him back was how could he die with an unfinished novel or sequence of poems in the files? This was vanity again as if the world were waiting for his books. Perhaps it was also the influence of religion. Why think you are more important than other creatures? Where is the evidence? If you study the universe and history long enough you are bound to see we're all up for grabs including writers and their noteworthy lack of humility. He had long known that humility was the most valuable characteristic you could have. Otherwise you would be a victim of the vain dreams and ambitions of youth. Whoever told writers they were so important in the destiny of man? Shakespeare and a very few others qualified but thousands and thousands of others dropped into the void without a sound. It reminded him, oddly enough, of the day he interrupted his work for a while to try to help a trapped wasp behind a light window shade in his studio. The wasp drove him batty in its fruitless struggle to get through the glass back to its nest in the apple tree twenty feet from the window. He was finally successful though the wasp was

furious at being caught and wagged its lethal tail trying to
sting him. When he released it out the door it flew straight
toward the apple tree. Despite being a lifelong hunter he
wasn't up to killing the wasp but then there were days he
couldn't swat an ordinary, irritating housefly. Who was to
say they were less important than a writer struggling for
fame? He filed this in his head under *reverence for life*, then
was embarrassed as the phrase seemed pretentious. He paid
the farmer to come over and file down the teeth of the piglets
so they wouldn't injure their mom when sucking. His wife
was pleased with the gesture but he said it was pro forma.

Because he wasn't visiting the bar he had bought a dozen
shooters for his studio. However with the decline of his drinking his tolerance had diminished as well and a shooter was too
much a hammer to the temple. At the wine store he bought
several bottles of Brouilly, a light French red he had drunk
in bistros on his several trips to Paris. He ordered a case as a
reward for quitting the bar in favor of his piglets. He stopped
to see his friend and neighbor in town and brought along a
bottle of Brouilly. His friend said, "Too cool today. That's a
warm weather red." He felt a bit rejected but respected his
friend's greater knowledge. He was quizzical about how he
could afford an expensive wine every day.

Back at the studio, after he had fed the sow, he struggled again with names for his piglets, ignoring the adage
that farmers don't name animals they're going to have to kill
one day. In his current good mood every creature on earth
was going to live forever which signaled a manic plunge.
He thought of naming the largest male Aristo after Aristo-
phanes's statement "Whirl is king" because the male whirled

at top speed when he wrestled the other pigs. The shortest, fattest male he named Chuck simply because he looked like a Chuck. He named one of the females Shirley after the piglet his grandfather had let him name, then labored over other possible names and failed. This was a case where he had to be precise.

He called his wife's cell and said he was tired and would sleep on the cot in the studio. He drank a modest twelve-ounce glass of red wine to aid sleep. He turned on his night-light and flopped on the cot with a twenty-year-old sleeping bag like a child's favorite blanket.

At 3:00 a.m. he awoke with a jolt and yelled. The minstrels had invaded his dreams again. He hadn't had a recurrence of the dream in years and now this was twice in a few months. He was horrified. They were singing loudly a few feet from his face and he couldn't move. He yelled, "Stop it!" as loudly as he could and they slowly withdrew into darkness. He turned on the lights and sat down at the safety of his desk and doodled a drawing of the layout of the farm he wanted to buy. There would be sixty acres of field corn for the pigs to eat and forty acres of well-fenced pasture with a small woodlot for them to frolic in and vastly increase their flavor. The bland-tasting pork at the supermarket comes from confined pigs in the big factory farms. He saw himself clearly in the future as the prince of free-range pork. He cautioned himself unsuccessfully against this obvious mania. The unlocked front door of the studio opened. It was his wife holding the cocked revolver.

"I got up to pee and heard you yelling. I thought you might need help."

"How touching," he said sincerely and took the proffered pistol, carefully easing the hammer down so she couldn't kill him by mistake.

They made love for the first time in nearly a year. He remembered again how wonderful it used to be, so much better than stray lovers because you don't know each other's bodies. You can't truly cozy up to a stranger except mechanically. She wanted something to drink and he had a small can of V8 which he poured into a plastic glass with some ice and a shooter. He drank a shooter straight from the little bottle.

"How can you do that?"

"I've had plenty of practice." He turned on the outside light so she could look down at the pigs. They were nursing for a middle of the night snack.

"I don't like them but I admit the little ones are cute. I have to leave. I'm getting up at four a.m. to go to a horse show over in Whitefish."

"Buy one on me."

"Thanks but I have enough horses. When I was a kid I heard about a farmer who died of a heart attack in a pigpen and his pigs ate him."

"That's a lie. I researched that story which everyone's heard and there's no truth to it."

"Defend those you love." She kissed him goodnight and was off into the dark which she feared less than he did. His life was full of imagined monsters.

He tried hard to sleep, always a failure when you try too hard, then got up and made instant coffee and had another shooter. He wanted to be conscious but not too much so.

He looked down at his clumsy drawing of the farm and his mind began to whirl. Enough of this farm that doesn't exist!

His most irksome item of late was and continued to be his fifty-year slavery to language. He had read Keats at fourteen and the guillotine fell. He was no longer free but an addict of poetry. He recalled sitting on the roof looking at the stars and a new moon the night of his birthday, December 11. Poetry requires vows and he made them. Much later, seven years to be exact, his father and sister died in a car accident. After this the vows became harder than marble. If this can happen to those you love any other work is unworthy. When he started writing prose too, at first it felt like he was committing adultery, but he soon recognized that if he was working on a novel he also wrote more poems. Poetry started the workday. Pasternak told us, "Revise your souls to frenzy." No matter how his life was compromised he kept at it, even on visits to Hollywood he was a servant of poetry. Los Angeles isn't a city of early risers so his habitual morning walks were unpopulated. Across from the hotel where he always stayed, the Westwood Marquis, was the splendid UCLA botanical garden which he loved to daily distraction. There he would often meet a Chinese surgeon who sat quite motionless beside the pretty carp pool to prepare himself for six hours of brain surgery. He himself was prepping for a day of meetings that would help no one but a few who needed money, including himself. The irony was he was getting $350,000 for his next screenplay, a first draft and a set of changes, enough to buy the small farm he had been imagining.

When they first moved out of town his wife had criticized him for peeing outside. He had responded, "Farmers pee outside." He had lived on his grandpa's farm when he was young and his father couldn't find work in the late years of the Depression. "I thought you were a writer," she had responded, meanly he thought. The irony was that that was a great deal of money for something he could write in a month. He knew he would shut off the water if he wrote too fast and a bit clumsily but it was fun to make that kind of money quickly when in his teens he had done a number of jobs for anything from sixty cents to a dollar an hour which he still resented years later. If you unload a fertilizer truck in a hot shed for eighty cents an hour you remember it. He worked alone. There were four tons of fertilizer in bags and even his trousers became soaked with sweat. He drank a quart of cold water afterward and collapsed on his ass in a faint. Now he thought it might have been good for his writing. He had known another reality. At some point he slept again.

A few mornings later he got up at the first bright sun shining through the studio window. He turned on his little electric water pot and made a cup of instant coffee. It was wretched, though in general better than it used to be. Some progress on earth. He went outside, peed, and bowed deeply to the grave of Alice.

He was excited because this was the first morning he was going to try to take a piglet for a walk. He had no idea what would happen, cautioning himself that they were scarcely puppies.

He reached over the side of the pen and grabbed Walter, a medium-sized male, who always seemed a little dim-witted and slow. Walter walked ten feet from the pen then turned and looked back into the pen at his mother who was watching and cried piteously. Walter wouldn't work out. At this point he was still a mama's boy. He looked at Shirley whom he thought of as queen of the litter. She was alert, independent, a little fierce and feral. She would drive others into a corner in order to nap in peace. Sometimes she would punish them with bites. She was always scrappy and would gratuitously bother the others. She always hogged the best teat. He dropped the limp Walter into the pen and Darling nuzzled him in consolation. He grabbed Shirley who seemed to have a "choose me" attitude. The moment he put her down she was off and running like a bat out of hell. She headed for a boulder in a thicket in the far corner of the pasture as if she had been studying the location from the vantage of the pen for a long time. He trotted after her, tripping on a rock, and painfully knocked out his wind. His wife was watching from her flower garden.

"Are you okay?" she yelled.

"No, bring Mary."

"What's wrong?"

"Bring Mary. Shirley is loose."

He was sitting up now, coughing from his last hundred cigarettes. Mary was a well-trained black English cocker spaniel who would go out and herd a horse back to his wife when she wanted to ride. Mary would visit the pen and growl and all the pigs would back up except Shirley who would stand nose to nose with her at the fence ignoring the growling as if she could tear the dog apart.

When his wife arrived with Mary he was still sitting on the ground struggling to get his air back. He wasn't used to moving quickly. While other men ran he walked, thinking a couple of hours of walking every day made up for the difference in immediate exertion.

Mary spotted Shirley rooting in the far bushes near his sitting rock and seemed to understand her mission. She headed toward Shirley at a dead run with his wife in chase. His wife could run doing so every morning. Shirley turned around and faced the oncoming yipping dog. They were immediately a ball of fur, pink fat, and muscle. His wife grabbed Mary's collar and Shirley ran for the other far corner. Mary twisted away and gave chase. Mary was running between the fence and Shirley, crouching her body and trying to herd her up toward the pen. He guessed Shirley would get tired, not being used to running. At that point Shirley suddenly stopped and sat down. Mary with her tongue way out sat down about five yards away from Shirley. He and his wife got there at about the same time.

"My poor baby is bleeding." A little blood dripped from Mary's ear.

"You could tell they weren't kissing," he said.

"You asshole."

He threw her a kiss then leaned and picked up Shirley setting her in his arms on her back which makes piglets passive. He carried her to the nearby pen and leaned over dropping her a short distance. She immediately returned to glaring out of the pen at Mary who had come over to growl.

A week later he was still ignoring his life's work in favor of tending to the pigs though it seemed that they had no need for him except food. Mealtime is a time of great excitement for pigs. There was an absurd misadventure when their water tank overflowed while he was on the phone with a New York editor. He returned to find the pen a mud hole which was aesthetically displeasing. He got a tub from the work shed near the house and filled it with warm soapy water. The piglets were fairly cooperative when he washed them off except Aristo and also Walter, who had become more animated with Aristo's influence. He scrubbed the mud off Aristo who faked placidity, then suddenly jumped out of the tub and ran for it. When he lunged for Aristo, Walter also jumped out and chased after his mentor. He hollered at his wife who was planting her vegetable plot's early lettuce and peas. He added, "Bring Mary" in a shout. She came a little slowly and Mary immediately saw the piglets trying to hide in the bushes near the big rock. There was no violence this time though Shirley jumped straight up and down in the pen in excitement. Mary expertly herded Aristo and Walter back to the pen. They were sparkling clean and air dried.

"They're just going to muddy themselves again," his wife said.

And so they did with evident pleasure. His effort had been futile.

"There's a chemical I put in the tub that prevents a pernicious skin rash, sometimes fatal." He was lying.

She suspected as much but humored him. "I'm not eating any dirty pig. They look better clean."

"Pigs have a right to get muddy. It's the main pleasure of their lives." He asked himself why he was arguing with her when he had just spent the afternoon washing piglets.

"How do you know? Maybe it's sex."

"They don't think about sex in advance like us. They just do it," he said with a bit too much authority.

"Now you're a swine psychiatrist?" she said with a withering touch. She left for her garden.

Walter and Aristo had returned to the mud hole with gusto, their eyes blinking out below muddy brows. He picked up Marjorie who was pretty clean thanks to some still dry straw in a corner. Of all the piglets she liked most to be touched. He picked her up in his arms and she collapsed against his body as if they were lovers. He bathed her gently and put some fresh straw in her corner. She curled up in pleasure to dry off. She fluttered her eyes at him and he couldn't help but wink. He took a little stroll with Marjorie and scratched her tummy.

Later he sat at his desk wanting very much to write a poem about piglets, not a comic poem. It would have to be a private poem for his eyes only because you need only to utter the word "pig" and some people would begin chuckling in their superiority. Pigs were of course edible but contemptible. He seethed in resentment in defense of pigs. The human race shits in its pants for at least the first year. Who else laughs in ridicule of fellow creatures? How could he write a poem if he was angry? Historians said that pork fueled the western movement. Without pigs there would be no west coast. Pigs would follow the wagon trains, their minds on a little corn for dinner. They would root for edible vegetables while cattle would wander off with their eyes on greener pastures.

He made a number of false starts on his pig poem then was so exhausted he drove to the saloon in town. Poetry does this to us. You can quickly either soar or drown in depression. You can have a pretty good first line but not a strong enough thought to tag along more lines and sometimes in the middle words become bored and make war on one another. Notebooks are full of these fragments, shrapnel of our intention. Life is short on conclusions and that's why it's often a struggle to end a poem. Some are lost forever. Sometimes you walk around with versions of a poem in your head that won't come clean. You are enslaved to this language of disorder and can brood upon it for days and weeks. When the poem finally does work, your spirit soars and you forget the difficulty, like you forget pain afterward. Some of the extreme behavior you see in the poet species is likely attributable to these struggles. When the brain spends this much time enfevered it is liable to affect the behavior which for a long period was a common joke around academia.

In down times of near clinical depression he wondered why he'd chosen this calling. Back at age fourteen when he was obsessed with Keats it seemed glorious despite the bad reviews Keats received during his short life. And Lord Byron had an enviable career of adventure and women, travel and women, poetry and women. And there was his beautiful rage when the Church of England wouldn't allow him to be laid to rest with his dog. If the minstrel couldn't be buried with his dog, he thought, he'd refuse to be buried. Just stick his body up in a tree and let him dry out in the wind. Pour out some good wine for the tree's thirsty roots. The nobility of dogs is unquestionable compared with men. He meant at some point to write a novella called "The Dogs of Jesus." Maybe it would be in the voice of the dog who was with him for his forty days in the wilderness.

Ralph, another wine-drinking neighbor in town, over a bottle of Châteauneuf-du-Pape had described rather too eloquently how writers make up their lives with language and then are obligated to live them. They are absurdly autonomous. He felt resentment over this easygoing indictment and reacted with a brisk, "How do you know?" But Ralph did know and said he had published two novels and a book of poetry in his twenties and then quit in a state of boredom with himself. This seemed unlikely but Ralph admitted he should have held on because writers had the advantage of surprise in life. They got to discover what they were going to write next. Ralph's father as a hard-ass business executive wouldn't support him as a writer but the money would keep coming if he took a Ph.D. which back then would ensure future employment. His father had come to maturity in the Depression and was a maniac worrying about money. And so Ralph took a Ph.D. which required years of semi-indolence. He studied the medieval literature of Europe for which he had no real passion but its distance from his emotional life made it safe. Only it wasn't. He became fascinated with the jongleurs, the medieval French poet minstrels who worked outside the Church and became a symbol of ultimate freedom in an authoritarian society. In a way they were bums living by their wits with an Indian trickster's ability. He stayed in Montpellier for years, learned the difficult language of the poets, and lived down the street from the university where the great Rabelais had been educated in the sixteenth century. He was enamored with southern France in the 1950s with so many of the remains of the war visible. People were happy just to be alive. His professors were a bawdy and good-humored group of ex-officers with totally laissez-faire attitudes toward him as an academic. When millions die around you who gives a shit? Ralph himself became his own kind of jongleur and always carried himself lightly. When he married a French girl it was a very good marriage but she died giving birth to their only daughter. To the disappointment of her parents he raised the daughter in the countryside of North Carolina. They tried to get a legal injunction against him taking the daughter out of France but it wasn't possible. They visited America every year to see their only grandchild. He had inherited a generous amount of money from his obnoxious father. He would take them all to a resort on vacation after doing research to make sure the food was good. The elderly French couple liked a dude ranch near Livingston, Montana, which was how Ralph had ended up there, and once when he screwed up dates for summer flights they came in December and they all stayed at a dude ranch near Patagonia, Arizona, where winter was sunny and passably warm.

During his early pig obsession he had missed the wine and company of his neighbors.

Chapter 3

He sat in front of the studio in his cheap white plastic chair and stared as he always did at his wife's vegetable and flower garden. She grew the two together. A simple plot of vegetables but the mixture of flowers made it lovely.

His problems were immense. It was May and the piglets were all over forty pounds. Zack came over and they enlarged the pen. None of the piglets were glad to see them anymore unless they were bringing food. He was distressed and he said to Zack, "What do I do now?" and Zack replied, "Lots of parties now at the end of the university semester. Sell them for pig roasts on the hoof." He made Zack a fine deal that if he sold the pigs he could keep half the money. He decided to keep Marjorie and of course the old sow no one would want. The next day he saw the ad Zack had called in to the university newspaper that began with, "The best pork you will ever put in your mouth. Perfect size for roasting."

Two days later Zack came over with his pickup the back of which was covered with a truck cap. He was a big strong former farm kid and loaded the piglets except for Shirley who he had to half strangle to get into the back of the truck. She nipped his hand pretty hard. "Got 'em all sold except for one. I'll cook that one myself. You'll be invited." He said, "No thanks," with a ghastly lump in his throat. How could he eat one of his pets? He was truly an amateur as a farmer.

Now that he had raised pigs the only consequential fantasy of his youth left to him was to live in France. He had saved all his earnings from age thirteen to eighteen to live in France, thirteen hundred dollars in all. A scoundrel eye doctor checking his sight said that he might be able to restore some sight in his blind left eye. His parents had no insurance that would cover this previous injury and no money what with a modest salary and five children. Being able to see out of the left eye was a more immediate temptation than France so when the surgeon asked what kind of money he could raise he stupidly said thirteen hundred. The surgeon said he would do the operation at that discounted price plus throw in a contact lens to help it work. It didn't work at all and the lens also was worthless and painful. He threw it out in the swamp behind the house. He was destined to always see a dense fog bank, unconsoled when he discovered that holding the lids open he could see a small light in the sky. He had spent his life savings for France on an utter failure. Later on another eye doctor said the surgery was "criminal."

Not surprisingly he entered a depression. His girlfriend abandoned him because she wanted to get married right after high school graduation. He was an ace debater but couldn't talk her into sex without marriage. The loss of this girl and France at the same time prolonged the depression. In fact on his senior trip by train from Michigan to New York City they had stopped in Niagara Falls and on a very high bridge across the river for the first time he thought deeply of suicide. What prevented him from the fatal act is that he didn't want to upset his parents or brothers and sisters who apparently loved him as he did them.

He never quite escaped this darkness but it was a small problem that his poetic thoughts about death were often disturbed by the fact that he was hungry. Maybe he should eat something first and then commit suicide. He had always kept this a secret only and inevitably thinking of it when he had a minstrel dream. The only good thing about the minstrel dreams is that they detoxified the suicidal mind-set by inspiring such hatred. The other and more long-ranging effect of the minstrel nightmare was of course that he forever quit doing poetry readings. He didn't unlike so many others see the connection between performance and poetry. Some poets seemed to take to it quite naturally, grinning and chuckling over their own dark witticisms. He had always thought that a Native American should have shot Robert Frost for the outrageous lie of the line "The land was ours before we were the land's." What a scandal that would be, America's best-loved geezer falling in a battle over poetry.

Chapter 4

Raising the pigs had given him the courage to plan an extensive trip to France. He had by now been there several times but always for overplanned trips for his French publisher Christian Bourgois. They were full to the hilt with interviews and bookstore signings with very little time for the general wandering around that he valued so highly. He later reflected that these were exactly like American book tours except the food was wonderful and Paris itself was more fascinating than any American city. For reasons completely unclear to him the French had taken kindly to his work and soon his French sales exceeded those in the United States which had never been all that good. He was reviewed widely and well but that had never translated directly to the cash register. It had always amused him that publishers like movie companies would never know sales in advance.

He wanted to be aimless in France. A month might do it and he would stay longer if he wished. He wanted to go to Toulouse and eat as much as he could of the bean stew cassoulet, which would be a lot, and to the seaport Marseille, and to Arles which he knew of by having read about the lives of van Gogh and Gauguin. Of course they had lived together but it hadn't worked out because van Gogh's instability exceeded Gauguin's. He cut off his own ear which made some biographers sympathetic saying that he did it for love, in itself incomprehensible. No one cuts off his nose for love.

Thinking over his short trip to Paris he mostly recalled lunches and dinners and getting over them. He would rise early, usually because of jet lag, and walk for an hour or so until a café opened where he could get an omelet with lardons (pork morsels) after which he would rest, then walk another hour to stimulate his appetite for lunch, then a long nap, and another longish walk and a couple of glasses of red wine. Hard liquor was too expensive. He had been hungry the afternoon before and had stopped at the Ritz for a fifty-dollar chunk of foie gras and two forty-dollar glasses of burgundy. It was just what he needed after crossing the bridge and walking in the Tuileries. The tab was a hundred and thirty dollars to which he added a twenty-dollar tip. While walking back across the river he thought it over and once again decided that he had no meaningful comprehension of money. He had stayed in the Ritz once for several days in the early 1990s. It was the anniversary of *Le Nouvel Observateur* and everything was billed to the magazine. Allen Ginsberg was also a guest and called one morning to complain that two eggs were forty dollars on the room service breakfast menu. He told Allen that it was on the house and Allen had said, "I don't like the idea," and he agreed. "Me neither. Back home farm eggs are two bucks a dozen. I could be eating twenty dozen eggs at this price." You simply ate the hotel eggs and regretted it in the name of the poor.

He was brought up in modest circumstances but his wife's parents were well off if not wealthy. His wife kept a sharp eye on their budget. She said she didn't "connect" with his newfound wealth when the screenplay money started rolling in. She continued on in her usual modest way though he paid fifteen grand for a horse she had been wanting that reminded her of *Black Beauty*. He had no particular interest in horses but this one was gorgeous and would follow him and the dog as they walked in the pasture. Now he often walked Marjorie, the only piglet left. She was slow because she sniffed at everything like a bird dog. One day she flushed a covey of Hungarian grouse and he liked the idea that Marjorie would work as a bird dog.

His wife kept warning him that his newfound prosperity couldn't last forever and that he should save more of it. He ignored her. In truth spending a lot of money put him off balance though it didn't quite sound an alarm. He was transparently a financial nitwit. He spent way more than sensible redecorating the house, spent lavishly on meals in New York and LA, spent on cars, hotels, pointless travel, fishing in Mexico and Costa Rica. When the air cleared, though it was still fuzzy, he figured he had loaned out more than $250,000 and had got only the two thousand back from the Indians. This only served to make him sensitive to the fact that he was stupider than he thought.

The real hurt, though, came when he understood that he was overlooking his true work, poems and novels, to make more money writing screenplays. This happened only twice after he quit teaching for good, and he immediately wrote harder, ten hours a day, seven days a week. Naturally he got tired and the only thing that saved him was taking his bird dog and some groceries up to a reasonably remote cabin he had bought on his splurge near the harbor town of Grand Marais in Michigan's Upper Peninsula. The cabin drew him back to his youth when he was seven and his father and two uncles built a cabin on a lake for a thousand dollars in used lumber, a wonderful cabin only twenty miles from Reed City where his father worked as a county agricultural agent. His family lived there all summer long. Sometimes he rode to work with his father in order to make a little money weeding gardens, mowing lawns, washing cars. On a good day he could make two or three dollars. He would come home and swim, eat some dinner, and go fishing for bass in the evening. On good days when he didn't work in town he would catch a pile of bluegills his family loved to eat. This was how he was slowly led to his life as a passionate fly fisherman. It's not just catching fish but the delicacy and grace with which you catch them. Not big hooks, hurtful to the fish, but tiny flies with tiny hooks.

He wondered now if there was a short course on money. The economics course he'd taken in college was now a burned-out lightbulb and all that he could recall was the course made actual money seem abstract. It wasn't. It was either in your pocket or not in your pocket. Years ago when he first started getting bigger money he got some local accountants and lawyers involved in his problems including taxes. They were very smart men but overly admired his earning power. This was comic. He traveled frequently to LA and New York to work on screenplays and stayed in high-rent hotels. In the mornings outside his door there were always copies of the *New York Times* and the *Wall Street Journal.* The latter was new to him and could have been in Latin. He kept at it and memorized enough financial gibberish that the hometown accountants presumed he was money smart not understanding that there was no background of knowledge to what he said or noting that the balance sheet made it clear he was guilty of slippery malfeasance. For instance, he hadn't filed a tax return for a decade and when they got him out of that one the fines were several thousand dollars. He went merrily on trying to ignore his leaden heart and feet. He could now afford all of the cocaine and best booze extant, a surefire combination for causing depression. The depressions were horrid indeed and the only way he could handle them was poetry and walking them off in the uninhabited paths of the Upper Peninsula. He could walk days on end without seeing a single person until he returned to Grand Marais and the saloon. His bird dogs Sand, Tess, and Rose loved it and so did he except for the exhaustion.

One very warm July day he got up at dawn to take advantage of the cool air that wasn't there. He swore to finally put an AC unit in his studio. He had an odd sense of foreboding having experienced a few minutes of minstrels in his dreams. He went out to feed Darling and Marjorie and discovered Darling to be dead and Marjorie quite ill. His wife was having coffee in her robe on the front porch. He hollered strongly and she came halfway down with Mary in alarm.

"Call the county agent. Darling's dead and Marjorie's sick."

She ran to the house while Mary entered the pen, sniffed, and shied away from Darling, then licked Marjorie's ears. They had lately become ardent playmates. Marjorie's eyes fluttered and he was relieved she wasn't dead. Naturally he wept, the mother of good things was dead.

The county agent, Winfield, got there in an hour. He knew him fairly well and at first he misunderstood his gruff, laconic nature though there was always a twinkle in his eye. He asked to see the feed, ran it through a hand, staring at it closely.

"It's mycotoxins, badly moldy grain. It's my fifth case with fatalities. I warned the grain elevator to alert their customers. They must have forgotten you."

"Why didn't Marjorie die?"

"I don't know. She probably didn't eat much or she'd be gone too."

A small lightbulb went off and he said that on their morning walks Marjorie dug and rooted a lot in an old garden spot. Recently she had demolished a whole row of turnips and several rutabagas and now was working on horseradish root. He said he'd tried to stop her, thinking that horseradish root would be too hot and spicy.

"Pigs don't give a shit," Winfield said. "You could pour a whole bottle of horseradish on a ham from their mother and they'd eat it."

He was mystified when Winfield knelt and closely examined Marjorie. "She's sick but she'll pull through. Give her a couple of quarts of milk." Mary growled at Winfield as if he might be hurting Marjorie.

"They think they're in love," he explained, a little embarrassed by Mary's behavior.

"I know an old baloney bull who made friends with a barn cat. They hung out together all day. The cat sleeps on the bull's back and sometimes just rides around. If we got close to this bull or his cat friend we'd get our asses kicked."

He called Zack who brought over his big backhoe and buried Darling fairly close to her daughter Alice. His heart ached when Zack dragged her over the lip of the hole and she made a mighty thump when she landed at the bottom. Zack had a few dairy cows and brought over a half gallon of milk for Marjorie. She drank hungrily sharing some with Mary. He was charmed watching the lovers drink together, their heads touching.

Zack had a pint of whiskey in his coat and they sat on the studio steps looking at the raw grave drinking the whiskey straight from the bottle. It was cheap and made them cough but then some think raw booze is a pleasure. His old Finnish friend in the Upper Peninsula thought that any sort of mixer was a waste of time.

Chapter 5

Breathing in and out is problematic in marriage. The early surge of ardent love wanes and flags. They had had a fairly low period after he taught at Stony Brook on Long Island. His wife didn't care for it there, lonesome for a couple of horses she had stashed in Michigan. She had recurrent nightmares of sheep in burning boxcars. There was also the idea that on Long Island they would be trapped in case of nuclear attack. This was at the height of the Cold War and Long Island also began to further his claustrophobia, a lifelong infirmity. The screenplay work was thin, but a boon happened when he received a grant of a year's living expenses from the National Endowment for the Arts. When they'd spent the last of that money in Key West, they returned home to a letter at the post office saying he had won a Guggenheim Fellowship. He had been promoted in his absence at Stony Brook but his wife didn't want to return to Long Island which she saw as unspeakably dense and overdeveloped. And he was fatigued with being a college poet and living up to the cliché of being a drunk and a womanizer. He did a good job at it but it was relentlessly phony.

So they stayed in northern Michigan at the time on their little farm for which a friend had loaned them the down payment. The farm was nineteen thousand and the mortgage was only $99 a month. Still it was a struggle. At the time he received only five thousand dollars for a novel which didn't work. He did some informal sports and outdoor pieces for *Sports Illustrated* and other magazines. It was hard to get enough money together to get a drink. They went insecurely from month to month in a very nearly squalid condition. He did eventually have to return to teaching but the objective was to put it off as long as possible, preferably forever. The good parts were a fine garden spot and a big barn on the property. He loved the barn because it reminded him of his not so idyllic youth. They boarded three huge draft horses and two saddle quarter horses for some extra income. One of the draft horses was the Midwest's largest, a mare named Sally who weighed twenty-six hundred pounds. She was like having a grand painting out the kitchen window in the back pasture. He took to wearing bib overalls like an actual farmer. Later they began referring to their penury at the time as "the macaroni years." He had forbidden her to accept any money from her parents though they were ready and willing to help.

In his writing downtime fooling with the pigs he had evolved a theory, not ready for release, he called a "glimpse." The word was not quite right but would have to serve for

the time being. In short it was typified by the way reality
can break open and reveal its essence like bending linoleum
until it broke and then you saw the black fiber underlying it.
Standing on the bridge at Niagara Falls tempted by suicide
was such a moment. Or holding Alice's little dead body before burial. In both he had seen altogether too poignantly
the sweep of life. Death gets your attention. He felt a little
of it riding in a friend's Ferrari going 160 miles per hour
on a freeway. That however didn't make his definition. It
was too contrived and foolish. Once in a bar in Key West
he was sitting at the end of the bar when two quarreling
Cubans pulled pistols. He dropped to his knees silently,
crawling through the kitchen and out the back door where
he hid in a hedge smoking for a half hour. He would always
remember what the bartender said when he went back in:
"Ramon was pissed. He said he would kill him and by golly
I bet he will."

     His father had some Mennonite second cousins he liked
and his family stopped to visit them now and then when
they drove south in Michigan. This group of Mennonites
lived on big farms near Ithaca. He was fascinated with these
people knowing that they didn't drink, smoke, dance, listen to radio, or have a TV. They almost never showed any
sexuality except in sort of an underneath way. He was about
twelve at the time and was just beginning to feel his first
strong hormones. Every time they stopped by he felt sweet
on a girl named Ruth about his age. She was so demure and
shy it was next to impossible to get her to say anything. She
wore a long gray dress and her little black skullcap which

was obligatory. One afternoon she approached the driver's side of their parked car where he was sitting and listening to the Detroit Tigers play the Yankees on the radio. She drew quite close considering it was against the rules for her to listen to a radio. In an act of uncommon bravery he reached out the window and took her hand. She was startled but she didn't withdraw her hand which felt oddly strong for a girl's. She let her hand go limp.

"Will you marry me?" he said as if acting in a play.

"I can't marry outside the church," she said softly.

"Then I'll become a Mennonite," he insisted.

They both laughed at his absurd earnestness.

"Let's take a walk," she suggested.

He turned off the radio and followed her into the barn where she showed him a very young draft horse filly. "My dad called her Ruth after me."

He felt the filly's feminine soft nose and scratched an ear. She was beautiful. He followed Ruth out into the main barn away from the stables. She began to climb the ladder up to the mow.

He nodded and climbed after her. They were violating a farm kid joke about the boy always trying to get a girl to go up the ladder first so he could see her legs. He wondered if she knew the joke. Her black socks went above her knees and then there were the two bare thighs. In the dim light of the barn he couldn't see between the thighs. He felt a weakness in his shoulders as if he might not be able to climb the ladder. At the top she flopped back on some loose hay blushing furiously.

"You were supposed to go first."

"I know it," he said boldly. So she did know the joke. Her face was close to his so he kissed her on the lips. She held the kiss a few moments then pushed him away.

"I never kissed a boy who was outside the church." She seemed utterly jangled, the way he felt when he accidentally bit his cheek.

"I love you," he said.

"Don't say that you goof."

He never forgot this brief incident. It had followed him for over forty years like the minstrels only it was a good memory.

She pointed out a large hole in the floor telling him that every day at 5:00 a.m. she threw hay down to her father to give to the milk cows adding that her brother used to do it but he had run away the year before he became eighteen to join the navy and to see what she called the "seven seas." She stepped toward the ladder.

"No," he said. "I'm the man. I'm supposed to go first to catch you if you fall." She stopped unsure what to do in the face of his deviousness. He quickly stepped to the ladder and started down. She paused overlong so he stopped. He said, "Get started." She said, "Who cares?" and headed down. The view was clearer and lighter this time and he felt his poor body roaring. She stumbled slightly on the next to last step. He grabbed her and she slid the last few feet down through his arms. He hoped she didn't feel his trembling.

Outside her mother called from the back door of the house reminding her to feed the chickens. He helped, casting the cracked corn in a wide circle to avoid quarrels. Inside the cage she took a dozen eggs from the nest. He tried to kiss her again but she said, "No, please," looking at her feet. She ran to the house and he followed slowly carrying the basket of eggs.

That was that. The end of the story. When he explained his theory of glimpses he felt this was a good example. When his editor read it she wasn't all that impressed. "Where's the narrative? What's the story about? You promised when you sold the novel in advance that it would be a big sprawling story about love, lust, quarrels, and murder between three farm families, sort of a magnum version of *A Thousand Acres*." He couldn't very well admit that all of his ideas for a new novel had disappeared into raising a litter of pigs. Naturally he had been excited when he first mentioned the new novel and his editor was enthusiastic. He was very broke at the time and was getting that way again because of a very late Hollywood royalty check. His editor wrote him a quick note after their unpleasant phone confab. "For twenty-five bucks a reader doesn't want one of your *glimpses* but a big story right in the face."

This deflated him a bit though he knew very well writers in weak moments have always historically looked for philosophical underpinnings for their work. There were none that were not nearly laughable. Such campaigns were almost always led by the weakest writer in a group who had the most to gain, a fragile snippet of immortality as part of a "movement." The Beats were a different matter, he thought, with quite a bit of substance, especially in contrast to the academic poets they were departing from who reminded one of a corn patch in a drought year. Jack Kerouac's "automatic writing" worked if you were a good writer, otherwise it was gibberish. When he had tried it he came up with multiple pages about sex and food which was not surprising to him.

Despite the setback he could not shake his feelings about "glimpses." Maybe he could write such a book of vignettes if first he wrote a best seller and was back in her favor. Or when he went to France in a couple of weeks he would keep a journal of vignettes if they came to him in a foreign country, but why wouldn't they? It seemed like art blasphemy to wait, especially until you were old and rich, and the unlikelihood of them happening together struck his mood momentarily dumb. Writers are victims of their own goofy flights of the imagination. To have an imagination doesn't mean you have control of it. In his teens the mere thought of Ava Gardner's body made him erect. Why in God's name was she married to the loathsome shrimp Mickey Rooney when she could have him, he thought? Of course how could he afford her when he only made sixty cents an hour as a night janitor at the local college? What if she wanted a new Buick convertible and he couldn't afford a hubcap? Maybe he could win a lottery if he could find one. Michigan did not yet have a lottery. She would want a mansion if she didn't already have one with Mickey. Maybe she would be unfaithful to him with Errol Flynn or Tyrone Power or, more likely, Cary Grant. To become sodden and disarmed over the complications of getting Ava in his arms. Or Deborah Kerr tied to the stake in a nightie in *Quo Vadis*, or was it *The Robe*? Local girls were more reachable but were they suitable for a fifteen-year-old potential great artist? He was sweeping backstage one night when he saw a college

girl actress just standing there on the stage in her undies
looking out at the dark theater seats. He could think of nothing to say to her. She waved at him and he waved at her,
and then she walked through one of those theater set doors
that when you close the door the whole wall shudders. He
swept more quickly. If he couldn't say anything to this girl
with her beauteous butt what could he possibly say to Ava
Gardner? After he entered college the single most irritating thing people said was, "It's all in the mind." Of course
it was. Where else would it be? But they said it with insipid
incomprehension. What if he had followed the girl through
the fake door? She might start running for the police. He
couldn't permit himself the fantasy line she would perform,
"I've been waiting for you all my life." But this was reality
so neither of them said anything. This experience caused
him a great deal of unrest for weeks. The problem was that
it was an actual event and seemed to show him that he was
unprepared for a life of high romance. What would Lord
Byron have said but then it was unlikely Byron would be
sweeping auditorium floors. When he finally found a girl
willing to take his virginity he discovered he didn't know
how to go about it. She had whispered "go ahead" and they
continued necking and wrestling on a sofa. She finally took
charge and they were able to proceed. In novels couples
usually flopped back on waves of nothingness and the par-
ticulars weren't mentioned. He thought, with some help I
have solved the puzzle. It was more like the sensation of
melting than anything else. He expected dramatic changes
in his life afterward but nothing of significance happened.

Chapter 6

The toughest thing about his pig adventures coming mostly to an end was that he felt more obligated to be strictly a writer again. He searched through his messy desk ceaselessly looking for some notes for the presold novel. He was usually uncanny at remembering details but his idea had come along strangely in a troublesome dream at three thirty in the morning and retained a dreamy elusiveness. He had awoken with a jolt, had a drink from a pint on his desk, coughed convulsively, then dreamed of three cantankerous families that were neighbors down an imagined but very vivid gravel road. Their parked cars and pickups in the landscape were muddy and junky with evidence of many minor collisions. There was one very large barn between them and across the road a very large hay crop recently baled. In the dream all the people in the three narrow houses had a passing resemblance which indicated to him that the families were all related. The dream came with the conviction that they were all evil people except the children who continued being children in the malevolent atmosphere. All of them, especially the men, were profound boozeheads fueled by endless gallons of cheap vodka.

He liked the idea of evil rural families because the whole rural literary tradition in America had become buried in honeysuckle and lilacs, hardworking and noble yokels. He had lived all of his life in the country and knew that this was hopeless bullshit. It wasn't even fair to the rural people because it denied them their humanity making them comic book cutouts. It was the clear interface of ideology with fiction. Anyway, the whole idea had now dissipated.

He could always call his editor and ask for a copy of his original proposal but the idea was far too embarrassing because he had lied in his sales pitch and claimed to have written "a hundred pages" of notes for this new idea. The trouble with lying was how frequently you had to cover up for it. Sometimes you had to live the lie to prevent discovery that you had told it in the first place. What saved him was late that night he had yet another brief minstrel nightmare. His parents were holding him tightly because he was ill and shivering, but he had a miniature gun in his coat and was carefully shooting all the performers who would howl and drop to their knees with this acute form of a bee sting in the face. This image saved him because he dimly recalled his three farm families were severely alcoholic gun nuts imperiling his hero who lived downriver from them in his trout fishing cabin. Eureka! With guns and booze how could he fail? He had pretty much canceled the idea of France so

harsh was the idea of writing the novel after having lost the
story, so he was thrilled when his dream success revived it.
The idea of him going to France to write had been much
talked about for decades. He couldn't recall who had done
the talking but the idea was that looking back at America
from France you would see the home place much more lu-
cidly. He could put it off no longer and booked the tickets.
Of course the girl who brought him coffee every morning
in his inexpensive hotel would be seduced by him within a
day or two. How could she resist? A bold American artist
getting older but still in the arena.

In the past if he suffered a literary slight he reminded
himself that Melville had been forgotten for more than thirty
years. Writing like nature was full of unfairness. Hail killed
the baby warblers in their nest. Wars were obviously part
of nature and killed millions. What struck him about reading Anne Frank was not what everyone knew, that she had
died like millions of her relatives, but that she was obviously
destined to become a grand writer. The mortality of song-
birds hitting windows drove him crazy. You had a lovely
life ahead of you and then you struck a window and it was
over. The death of his sister at nineteen in an auto crash
with his father was still unacceptable fifty years later. It had
created its own nodule of permanent rage at the roots of his
consciousness. It was ultimately the cause of his becoming
a writer. If this can happen to those you love you may as
well follow your heart's wishes in your time on earth. He
found it quite comic when he realized that he had never
won an award that he had ever heard of before winning
it. "Here today, gone tomorrow," as people said. Ambition

grated while humility soothed. This was quite different from ambition for the work itself. All he would allow himself was the wish that his books stay in print. The aim was that when he was walking Mary and Marjorie in the morning he was simply walking a dog and a pig on a lovely morning not brooding about what a reviewer in New York had done to him. Once when he was washing popcorn butter off his hands in a movie theater bathroom there was a dapper young man next to him who was combing his complicated hair with amazing wrist flicks. He had dozens of waves and curls and smiled at himself in the mirror as he did it. He remembered thinking at the time that the guy was fucked for life. He might have a girlfriend who liked or loved his hair but not as much as he himself did. After the movie he saw the guy with a rather homely girl which made sense in that he wouldn't want to suffer by comparison.

Chapter 7

His month in France was a joy to the point that he later wondered why he came home. In every respect it was a feast for his senses and his naturally quizzical impulses. He had had a year of the French language but remembered next to nothing though a little seeped in from the past. It didn't seem to matter because all the French, at least in Paris, seemed to have enough English to bail him out of his minimal difficulties. An artist friend had told him about a wonderful room in a little hotel on Rue Vaneau which was near Rue de Sèvres and Rue de Babylone and only a couple of blocks from the Invalides, a handy landmark. There were small city maps free at the hotel desk and he was never without one. He got it out so frequently that it only lasted a few days before it would turn into soft pulp. He got into navigational trouble one day when he forgot his reading glasses and the map became a blur. He finally asked an old lady in a small park who gave him directions in clear English. They spoke a few moments and out came that she had been married to a soldier from Chicago. She lived with him there until the 1960s when he died and she moved home. She said she was tough because her parents were Basques. He didn't know what that meant but asked around and later found out. She took his shoulders and aimed him north toward the Tour Montparnasse, the only skyscraper on Montparnasse. From then on he would use the building as a beacon when he was confused. It was easy to take the proper right turn well before he reached the skyscraper.

Paris seemed to agree with his notion of glimpses. He walked hundreds of streets in the first two weeks until he got bad shin splints from walking on cement which his legs were unused to. He had to take a few days off, mostly made up of hot baths. He bought a pair of thick soft-soled shoes at Bon Marché and consequently discovered the immense food court on that floor. That helped. He skipped restaurants for a while. In the morning he'd buy the *Tribune,* have coffee, and then go into the food court, buy bread, a few cheeses out of the hundred they had, some pâté, salmon, and several kinds of herring. He vowed he would someday live nearby and cook in his own apartment out of this marvelous and expensive store. They had a big wine department but he preferred the small wine store across the street where he had gotten to know a friendly clerk. One day he bought on impulse a large double magnum of Mouton Rothschild but couldn't figure out what to do with such a large bottle so he took it to a dinner at his publisher's home who doubtless thought "Crazy American" and hid it from his current guests with glee. "A wine for the proper occasion," he said.

France brought back glimpses of his life of travel in the years when he was ever so slowly writing his most ambitious novel, screenplays, and also informal outdoor essays for *Sports Illustrated*. He went to Russia with a friend but their KGB guide didn't want him to write anything about Russian horse racing. He went to one race and saw Iron Jaw win. On the way home he stopped in France and wrote a piece about a stag hunt near a friend's family château. Of course he had never stayed in a château before but was comfortable as had been Richard III who had stayed there during the invasion of France. One evening he and his friend ate a wild piglet stuffed with truffles.

The same year, he and his wife went to Africa with the same friend and his wife, a grand trip. His biggest thrill was not the mammals, which he had seen so much of on television and in the movies, but the birds. Every bird in Africa was a bird he had never seen before including the large martial eagle who occasionally feeds on hyenas that weigh 150 pounds, just like Mongolian golden eagles can kill wolves. You imagine them dropping out of the sky the weight of a frozen turkey with huge talons. Bang. About anything is dead. He dreamed of returning to Africa simply to bird-watch by himself. He also traveled to Ecuador for a sporting magazine to catch a striped marlin on a fly rod. He succeeded finally on a later trip to Costa Rica.

Perhaps the most momentous trip in terms of long-range effect was a month in Brazil to research a screenplay for a producer. The constant presence of the music of Brazil seeped into the soul and could be recalled anytime. The thousands of beach girls were also memorable, their shapely bodies maintained by the endless physical beach games they play. One day he joined the tail end of an anti–nuclear weapons march led by a hot samba band. Everyone was dancing and he did the best he could. Finally one austere older woman, the soul of dignity, joined him and helped with dance steps. Afterward he asked if she would like to have a drink. She answered that if she had a drink with a strange man her husband would cut his throat. He found out later that many husbands in Brazil have the nasty habit of killing their wives. Farther north he loved the big former slave port of Bahia which was even more, if that was possible, musically saturated than Rio. It was intoxication without alcohol or drugs. Every kid sitting on a park bench strumming seemed better than any quartet he'd ever heard in the United States. In Bahia music was their life. There was no other. Maybe music was the only way to subdue the smothering poverty. You kept thinking of the music, the Atlantic Ocean in front of you, the night sky that opened people up rather than closing them. The dancing was ceaseless and he suddenly envied these people who danced every day rather than occasionally. More than once during his month he thought he might move there.

One grotesquely snowy December morning in Paris years before he had sat at his studio desk staring at an assortment of poems written since the last book of poetry three years before. This was when it was thirty rather than fifty years since he wrote his first poem while reading John Keats. Of course the poem was doggerel and he had known

it immediately. He thought of the thousands and thousands
of hours he had spent on poems since that calling at age
fourteen. "Calling" is sort of a theological term, as people
feel called to the ministry, and is less true of writing, but he
knew he had made a lifetime commitment. He was standing on the roof of the house in the middle of the night at
fourteen, staring at the Milky Way which seemed to stare
back with its fabulous plenitude. Now staring at the snow
thirty years later, he thought that his prose fiction seemed
more of an afterthought though he read a great deal of it.
He had to write and there were long periods of time when
he didn't have a poem ready to arrive. René Char, a French
poet he worshipped, had said about writing poetry, "You
have to be there when bread comes fresh from the oven."
You had to live your life in a state of readiness for the poem
even though it could very well be a month or two between
poems. Another pet obsession of his though not much believed in the cramped world of poetry was that every poet
is obligated to read everything published in poetry through
time, no matter from what country or time period. He spent
years and years doing so. How could you write if you weren't
familiar with what was best in the history of the world? He
went fishing and camping with friends at the cabin on the
lake where they brought piles of sex magazines to read while
he had only anthologies of Chinese and Russian poetry. He
didn't mind being teased about it because he was the biggest and strongest of the group and they went only so far in
their teasing for fear of getting their asses kicked. He was
an utterly nonviolent farm kid and just looked threatening

because of his musculature from a life of hard work whether bucking hay bales in tall stacks, unloading fertilizer trucks, or laying out irrigation pipe in the fields.

Recently while sitting in his studio watching his wife, a shapely woman indeed, work in the garden he had a few minutes of absolute happiness. He couldn't remember his last one, other than catching a five-pound brown trout in a local river. But this one was more solid and overwhelming. What happened was that he had a rapprochement with her after several years of growing distance.

It all started with smoking. She had had a severe asthma attack and spent a week at a hospital in Tucson. Her asthma was bad enough that she could no longer be in the company of anyone smoking cigarettes. Whenever he spent time in the house he was sequestered in his office, taping black plastic sheeting across the louver over the door. He was already claustrophobic and his dismal space considerably upped the ante. He couldn't face it, in fact. Maybe he would quit smoking. But then his singular success had been the seven weeks around spinal surgery. The surgeon told him for the sake of his healing bones he shouldn't drink or smoke for those seven weeks. He played the role of the hero and somehow managed without cheating.

They merged again one evening sitting on the porch swing watching fireflies and the thousands of stars above them, idly moving the swing back and forth with their feet. The night was unbearably beautiful with the constellations speaking their own strange language to each other. He told her he thought it might be the uninvented language used by Jesus and the Buddha to speak to each other.

"What a wonderful thought. I have to tell you something unpleasant. Your friend Ralph in town died this afternoon. I waited because I didn't want to tell you while you were enjoying your favorite lasagna dinner. His daughter is there on a visit. You should call her now."

He broke down weeping. He sobbed, in fact, thinking that his friend might have died of a heart attack while trying to pull the cork from a recalcitrant bottle of wine. He wasn't very strong. The two of them had recently been corresponding about Chinese poetry and he had begun to think of Ralph as his only true friend.

His wife held him and they sat there an hour vomiting up their souls, saying everything that was possible to say about their multiple faults that had kept them apart. Finally they made love to the obnoxious music of mosquitoes on the wooden floor of the porch.

Chapter 8

Long months of writing can pop your skull with strain. It's the tediousness of exhaustion he went through, the ache of a period wherein he wrote a novel quickly followed by a novella. It was a life of compulsion. He missed the variety of pigs and wandering around France. He still had Marjorie but Mary had a bad paw and couldn't walk. Marjorie had developed the illusion that she must look after Mary on walks rather than the natural vice versa. He figured that it was because she was conscious of her great size, probably about three hundred pounds he guessed.

One day he was walking Marjorie alone when the neighbor girl came past with her young German shepherd. The dog had likely never seen a pig before and scrambled under the fence in curiosity. The girl called out that her dog was "mean" and he yelled back, "So is my pig." Marjorie attacked the dog which snarled and barked. Marjorie pinned the dog in a corner with three fence posts. The dog was being strangled and crushed at the same time while its jaws were ripping at the pig's ears which she ignored. He tugged at Marjorie's neck but couldn't budge her. The girl tried to help but her skirt was caught in the barbed wire. He cautioned himself not to look up her lovely legs but to help her save her dog's life. He managed to wriggle and wedge a hand down between the dog and Marjorie and rip up whereupon he was able to toss the dog over the fence getting nipped badly in the shoulder in the process. The girl cringed in horror because his shoulder was bleeding though not as badly as the pig's ear. Meanwhile the dog headed home down the road at top speed. She embraced him. "Don't tell my father."

"Don't worry. I'm fine." He errantly let a hand slide down brushing her firm butt in the summer skirt. She trembled and so did his hand. She backed away, flushed.

"Why are we kissing?" she asked.

"Because we wanted to." He kissed her again even more passionately and clutching her rump. She wriggled and his fingers inched into the cloth-covered crevices. Marjorie made an alarming noise and they turned to her. She was clearly glaring at the girl. "Marjorie sit." Marjorie sat like a bird dog looking off as if embarrassed.

"I didn't know you could train a pig like a dog."

"It's one of my specialties," he said smugly.

"Maybe you could help me train my dog?"

"I'd be glad to."

"I better get home. They'll worry if I don't come back with the dog."

"One more kiss?" he said, pushing her a bit into the thicket that surrounded the big rocks down in the corner of the pasture. He began to lift her skirt.

She was frantic. "I don't take the pill yet." She squirmed loose and ran down the fence line.

He sighed and wondered how unlikely the whole thing was. She reminded him of a ripe peach.

His exhaustion made him feel inert. The one doctor was testing him for sleep apnea saying he wasn't getting enough oxygen when he slept. He didn't care what it was, he just wanted to be over it. He was inert with self-absorption, a detestable emotion where you only sat there thinking about your meaningless fatigue. He had been sleeping pleasantly with his wife since the death of his neighbor and the evening on the porch. She didn't feel up to making love but neither did he. He slept most of the day on his studio sofa, meaning a short nap that always elongated itself. The incident with the girl, her dog, and the pig was the only true lust he had felt for months.

Earlier in his career he had easily presumed that many of his problems were clinical and could best be handled by a battery of psychiatrists. Of late the exhaustion problem seemed insuperable. He read widely, as always, in the area of his problem which brought on the usual frustration of knowing what precisely was wrong and still being unable to do anything about it. After the doctors he slept most of a month. Quite suddenly he couldn't write a sentence but then he didn't want to. It was all he could do to sign a credit card receipt. When up he drifted as if sleepwalking mostly watching the multiple species of birds coming north from Mexico.

Fifteen years before, bored with northern winters, they had rented a house on a creek on the Mexican border. He hadn't realized that it was one of the prime bird areas of the United States but he happily assumed the childhood delight of identifying birds. He saw the rare Mexican blue mockingbird the first time it arrived there. The word got around and promptly there were literally hundreds of bird-watchers lining the fence crossing the creek on the property line. He was furious about the privacy invasion and told some of them that he was going to shoot the bird. A few women wept. He hung a sign saying, "Beware American Champ Pit Bull Black Savage." That definitely helped but not all that much. He drove to Nogales and went to Walmart and bought a boom box stereo and some CDs of the Mexican border featuring the music of love, violence, and death. That helped the most and seemed to frighten everyone. People would quickly come and go. He was amused that the Mexican blue mockingbird would prance up and down dancing on the boom box.

The whole area was gorgeous, mostly forested mountains and some desert all with both flora and fauna. A mother and daughter mountain lion had killed and eaten a deer in their brushy front yard. A jaguar was seen within a few miles of their house. Rattlesnakes were a bit of a worry. He had to shoot one in their bedroom one day. His wife had left the French doors open and the snake had come in to cool off. This was nothing compared with their warm weather place in Montana where a professional snake catcher had to remove a thousand rattlers in a cliffside den after he had lost his favorite English setter Rose. She had been bitten in the face with a fang protruding from her eye.

Earlier in his career when his writing had him well up a scrawny tree he was bright enough to take a break. He had been forced to admit that you can become stupider as you get older. During his Guggenheim year in his thirties he fished a hundred times but still managed to write a novel and a book of poems as the weather was bad frequently in northern Michigan.

Now, when his talent had etiolated, he often sat there suppurating, or worse yet simply dozed. He had always been a championship sleeper. Once he had taken two friends fishing and had fallen asleep in the act of rowing. When he had landed at de Gaulle in Paris a stewardess had to shake him awake. He was scarcely raring to go into a new life. Five cups of coffee and he could sleep immediately. He prided himself on being a good thinker whatever that meant. Not much most of the time. Luckily his memory had held out against attrition. He could see clearly backward into his waxing and waning. To wane was easy. Just come to a dead stop and you'll fall off the rails asleep.

Fishing, bird hunting, and cooking for years had been his central obsessions. Stop one and they all stopped. It was a mystery of sorts but more caused more. When he had become interested in cooking in those teaching years his wife was thrilled. There is scarcely a housewife who doesn't tire of coming up with something new every night for dinner. With him oddly it had begun somewhere between recipes and poems. In his usual state of hubris he decided to create original recipes that would amount to the size of a book of poems. Of course he quickly fell flat on his face. When questioned his wife would point out that his original recipe

wasn't original. She had a huge repertoire of recipes and a
library of cookbooks that impressed all visitors. Not having thought the problem through he was humiliated that he
wasn't a great creative chef instantly. She, meanwhile, was
highly amused to the point that he easily became quarrelsome. And to his despair he discovered that cooking and
drinking didn't go together, certainly not beyond a single
glass of wine.

His first victory was absurd. A young couple from the
French department had stopped by for a drink and to advise
him on his next trip to France. The young woman seemed
to know everything about food and wine. He did note how
quickly the young quiet and deferential man opened a bottle
of wine. It was enviable when he had seen it done in the
bistros and he thought it required big talent and an amateur
could never pull it off. His wife had warned him against
cooking from the books of Paula Wolfert as the recipes were
currently well "above his head." He had started a recipe the
afternoon before but it wouldn't be done until midnight. His
wife had made it once saying that he probably wasn't worth
all the effort. It was a stew made of duck legs and thighs,
garlic, thyme, Armagnac, and red wine. His wife was tired,
made an omelet with cheese, and went to bed, and he gave
up on the recipe.

Now they were all hungry sitting there eating olives and
drinking cheapish Côtes du Rhône, and the Frenchwoman
suggested they drive to their place across town and she could
whip up a little supper. He dramatically yelled stop and got
his half-finished casserole in its big blue Le Creuset from the
fridge. His wife said to her, "We'll heat it up. You'll probably

have to correct it." He improvised finishing the Cassoulet de
Canard and the Frenchwoman shrieked with delight, pro-
nouncing it beautifully on her sibilant tongue. After that he
would arrogantly try anything within or beyond his talents,
usually French but quite a bit from northern Italy and the
books of Mario Batali. He preferred the French but only
because they were more versatile. This food obsession had
lasted throughout his life, waxing and waning. A month of
intense activity might be followed by a month of laziness
with a few very simple Chinese meals thrown in. He loved
the way cooking took over his mind and resolved the usual
mental miseries which it always did. He suspected that it was
the root of his sanity if there was one which was doubtful.

The clearest mystery of his childhood was water which
led him to fishing. It was emotionally enriching like cooking
later became. You started by hearing from a teacher that
water was H_2O which never meant a thing. High on the
list of the loves in his life were rivers, the dozens he had
fished and others he'd simply seen on road trips. The good
fortune of his water obsession was growing up in northern
Michigan which abounded in wild waters, lakes, ponds,
creeks, rivers, and the Great Lakes. They visited the Great
Lakes on an occasional excursion where you couldn't see the
other side, and there was the feeling that there might not be
another side. His love of water became haunted from one of
the many fibs his older brother, currently a university dean,
had told him. His brother insisted that even puddles could
be bottomless leading down to China where you would be
beheaded with long swords like the Japanese did to GIs
during World War II, photos of which his mother had saved

from old *Life* magazines. Falling all the way through earth only to get your head chopped off was frightening indeed, the stuff of nightmares, but he realized his brother was just trying to scare him. His brother had also insisted that he had dreamed he would die in a river in South America strangled by an anaconda. This enormous snake captured his imagination at the Saturday afternoon serials at the movie theater in Reed City, in which a man named Frank Buck apparently had been attacked by every sizable creature on earth.

His lifetime of fishing began when he was about five and intensified considerably after his eye accident at the age of seven. His father had figured out that the only way to lift the melancholy of his little son was to take him fishing. They fished for trout on weekends on rivers when his dad was off work and during the week fished in the late afternoons and evenings at the cabin they lived at all summer long on a remote lake. His father and uncles built the cabin when the uncles returned from a very hard time in World War II in the South Pacific. He was impressed that they had built the lovely cabin for only a thousand bucks. The sound of rain on the tin roof was soothing to his eye which hurt a lot and after that he always identified a remote cabin with good feelings. A day never passed at the cabin without him fishing. Even when it was cold and windy he was bundled up and would let the wind carry him across the lake in heavy waters. Then he would have to strenuously row into the wind all the way home for dinner. Fishing was ordinarily not very pleasant in the high winds but he would screw up his eyes and imagine he was way up in Canada surrounded by polar bears.

He felt that rivers, birds, and forests had kept him alive and would continue doing so. His wife was far better than him at identifying birds but then she had far better eyesight. None of his friends were bird-watchers. They would try to tease him about the "sissy" sport. He would only answer obliquely that birds were the grandest facts of nature and life. When he was doing sports journalism fishing in Chile, Ecuador, Costa Rica, Nicaragua, Mexico it was altogether as pleasant as he thought it might be. He wanted to fish not write about fishing. It is often our conclusions that exhaust us. It also slowed him down that he had to hire guides for trout fishing because his vision was insufficient to tie on the tiny flies. Often, having a guide in the boat compromised the fishing. Guides want to talk about marriage and financial problems. He didn't.

He had also been impassioned with bird hunting for several years, especially for the grouse and woodcock, less so the quail and doves of the South. He never cared for deer hunting and had shot a deer only once which proved to be sufficient. It was unpleasant to gut and skin them, a moral exercise. They were wonderful to eat but he discovered that when he quit deer hunting plenty of friends shared their own kill including the antelope and elk of Montana.

He had trained half a dozen dogs which was more enjoyable than actual hunting. There was a mutual joy between them when the dog totally caught on to pointing the scent and then retrieving the bird. A momentary thrill, the total comprehension between dog and man over what precisely they were doing. His English setter Tess, a truly elegant creature, would often do a prancing dance after retrieving a bird. And when they began hunting she would often take off at a very formal gait similar to what you see in American Saddlebred horses. He loved poems that gave him goose bumps, and the same thing could happen hunting over a fine dog.

Obviously so much of the pleasure of hunting and fishing came from where you were. You were utterly enveloped in the natural world. Sometimes when he was trout fishing his mind played the cello. And sometimes when he would bird hunt for eight hours the exhaustion and also the taste of the French red wine when he got back to the cabin would be exquisite. He usually had two friends at the cabin and they would prep for dinner at midday break then slowly cook it when they got back to the cabin. They all cooked elaborately but sometimes they only grilled birds and would have them with a cheese polenta and lots of wine.

Passacaglia for Staying Lost,
an Epilogue

Often we are utterly inert before the mysteries of our lives, why we are where we are, and the precise nature of the journey that brought us to the present. This is not surprising as most lives are too uneventful to be clearly recalled or they are embellished with events that are fibs to the one who owns the life. A few weeks ago I found a quote in my bedside journal, obviously tinged with night herself, saying, "We all live on death row in cells of our own devising." Some would object, blaming the world for their pathetic condition. "We are born free but everywhere man is in chains." I don't believe I ever felt like a victim and so prefer the idea that we write our own screenplays. The form or genre of the screenplay is too severely compromised for honest results. You are obligated to write scenes that people will want to see, and "Jim, head in hands, spent an entire three days thinking" won't work. It's on the order of the oft-repeated slogan of the stupid, "I don't know much but I know what I think." Many years ago when I flunked out of graduate school, it occurred to me that the cause of this outrageous pratfall was the personality I had built. It all started when I decided at age fourteen to spend my life as a poet. There weren't any living examples in northern Michigan so I gathered what information I could, mostly fictional, and usually painters. Painters' lives can be fascinating, poets' less so. But both were at the top of the arts list. If I was tempestuous and living in a garret in New York or Paris I would look better with smears of paint on my rugged clothing than lint and dandruff. So I read dozens of books on poets and painters to give me hints on what kind of personality I should have. I even painted for nearly a year to add to the verisimilitude. I was a terrible painter, totally without talent, but I was arrogant, captious, and crazy so I convinced friends I was indeed an artist. This was just before the beatnik craze began, the motto being "If you can't be an artist, you can at least look like one." I tried to copy the paintings of old masters but on El Greco's View of Toledo I ran out of canvas halfway across Toledo. This was poor planning not poor art. What embarrassment though no one knew but my younger sister Judy who was into my art fever and burned red candles and played Berlioz while I worked. The model of course is the romantic artist, possibly the curse of my life in the way it tripped me and made me fall flat on my face over and over. Luckily my genetic mix of generations of farmers also gave me a desire for hard work so I was rarely unemployed. My dad said, "You'll always get by if you're a good shovel man."

The "everything is permitted" confusion has pretty much lasted my entire life. Of course it's nonsense but then the ego is beleaguered without its invented fuel and ammunition. You can't squeak out like a mouse that you're a poet, or walk in the mincing steps of a Japanese prostitute. Part of the trouble is that you are liable to think of yourself as a poet long before you write anything worth reading and *you have to keep this ego balloon up in the air with your imagination. I survived on both good and very bad advice. Doubtless the best is Rilke's* Letters to a Young Poet *and possibly the worst, which I religiously adhered to, was that of Arthur Rimbaud who advised you to imagine your vowels had colors and for you to go through the complete disordering of all your senses, which is to say you should become crazy. I managed quite easily. This was mostly to advise young poets not to become bourgeois. Even conservative old Yeats said that the hearth is more dangerous than alcohol. I feel recalcitrant about this having had a number of friends that are dead alcoholics. We've always lived rurally where it is much easier to avoid being bourgeois. The natural world draws you to herself with such power that you can easily ignore the rest of the culture and social obligations. When I was eighteen I found an Italian poet I liked, Giuseppe Ungaretti. He wrote,* Vorremmo una certezza *(give us a certainty), which is bad advice but understandable if you just lived through World War II. He admitted,* Ho popolato di nomi il silenzio *(I have peopled the silence with names). Also,* Ho fatto a pezzi cuore e mente per cadere in servitu di parole *(I have fragmented heart and mind to fall into the servitude of words). Of course. That's what you do. You might still be gibbering in your casket.*

All over America young people are going to bad writers for good advice. There are so many MFA programs in the colleges and there are not enough good writers around to teach in them. As opposed to what you might think, teaching is brutally hard work if you insist on doing a good job. And your own work is liable to suffer.

Money is the vicious whirl, a trap you are unlikely to live through in a healthy way. If you subtract screenplays I didn't make a living as a writer until my sixties. When I quit screenwriting to save my life my French rights moved in to save me.

In a lifetime of walking in the woods, plains, gullies, mountains I have found that the body has no more vulnerable sense than being lost. I don't mean dangerously lost where my life was in peril but totally misdirected knowing there was a lifesaving log nine miles to the north. If you're already tired you don't want to walk nine miles, much of it in the dark. If you run into a tree it doesn't move. I usually have a compass, also the sun or moon or stars. It's happened often enough that I don't feel panic. I feel absolutely vulnerable and recognize it's the best state of mind for a writer whether in the woods or the studio. Your mind feels a rush of images and ideas. You have acquired humility by accident.

Feeling bright-eyed, confident, and arrogant doesn't do this job unless you're writing the memoir of a narcissist. You are far better off being lost in your work and writing over your head. You don't know where you are as a point of view unless you go beyond yourself. It has been said that there is an intense similarity in people's biographies. It's our dreams and visions that separate us. You don't want to be writing unless you're giving your life to it. You should make a practice of avoiding all affiliations that might distract you. After fifty-five years of marriage it might occur to you it was the best idea of a lifetime. The sanity of a good marriage will enable you to get your work done.

Eggs

Part I

Chapter 1

Only later in life did she learn that chickens are the closest living relatives to dinosaurs. She found it hard to accept thinking we certainly aren't obligated to believe everything science tells us. It was anyway hard to imagine a dinosaur while watching a chicken eating scratch in the barnyard.

However, not quite as deep into the well of the past a small girl named Catherine was sitting on a milk stool in her grandparents' barnyard in Montana studiously watching chickens. She was in the second grade and had volunteered to write a report on the bird. Her classmates thought this was ludicrous. Why not report on horses or cows? Anything is more dramatic and interesting than an ordinary chicken. Families even kept chickens in the small village where Catherine lived only a half dozen miles from her grandparents' farm. Sometimes Catherine walked the six miles, mostly cross-country, to study the chickens. A seven-year-old girl wouldn't be allowed such a journey nowadays but back then it wasn't extraordinary. Boys played baseball all summer long into the evenings without organized teams or cute little uniforms. Girls went camping and fishing which they liked as much as boys, or rode their nags for long miles cross-country to go swimming. Parents didn't micromanage their children.

Catherine had three horses partly because of their need to keep one another company and partly because when it came to Catherine her father was a soft touch. They were kept at her grandparents' and to her disappointment the horses didn't care for chickens. They especially disliked the rooster Bob, who was arrogant and charged them crowing. He also charged Grandpa who kicked at him but rarely made contact because Bob was so deft. He was generally pleasant to Catherine seemingly thinking she was part of his brood.

Her grandmother was a bit capricious ordering chicks the post office delivered in a big box. Grandmother liked colorful feathers in her barnyard though she would get ordinary leghorns for reliability. The eggs were always white which Catherine's aunts favored. Her daffy older brother wouldn't eat eggs, odd for a farm kid but then he was a problem in every respect. That's why her father treated her like a son. Her grandpa's farm dog, a collie, used to retrieve the cows every day but thoroughly ignored the chickens though he would growl at the rooster if he approached which frightened the rooster. Grandpa only liked to eat brown eggs thinking they were healthier but then he was full of errant theories. Her father who was the banker in town said that this was because Grandpa was a Swede, and Swedes are known for their eccentricities. There were Rhode Island Reds and Plymouth Rocks for brown eggs, a few Golden Comets, a scattering of Anconas, and French Marans for variety and color. If you're a farm woman you struggle for anything different from the farm routines.

Catherine's father was American and grew up on the farm, while her mother was English. After he graduated from college he got a job with a big New York City bank with an office in London. He met her mother at a dance hall and he said that it was "love at first sight." Her mother was younger and impulsive and desperately wanted to live on a farm and he lied saying that that was where he lived though he had no intention of returning to farm life. So they married in England and came back home to Montana. She was plainly furious when they reached Montana and moved into a grand nineteenth-century home in the village. She simply asked, "Where's the farm you promised?" and he ignored her. She was already pregnant and knew she had to take his lie calmly.

When her parents quarreled which was frequently her mother would go out to his parents' and sleep in the small quarters she had organized for herself up in the cold attic in winter. She'd take Catherine along when she was small. In the winter she'd carry a large stone she had heated on the stove up to the attic, wrapped in a blanket to keep their feet warm. Everyone knew that if your feet were warm the rest of the body was easy with enough blankets. Of course by 5:00 a.m. their feet were cold but that's when her grandparents got up for breakfast to start the day. Catherine liked being with Grandpa at the kitchen table when he would sit waiting

for it to get light outside, a very long wait in the winter but
then the kitchen was warm from the wood-burning stove.
Grandpa would invariably eat a half dozen brown eggs,
ham or bacon or pork chops, and fried potatoes, also a bowl
of Wheaties with pure cream. It doesn't sound healthy but
he worked on the farm until he was ninety. He wouldn't
have a tractor, believing that motor exhaust poisoned the
ground, but plowed and cultivated with two large Belgian
draft horses. Once when Grandpa had pneumonia her dad
plowed the thirty-acre plot and was a physical wreck for a
week. He was so proud that he had done it and her mother
had to take many photos of the banker behind the plow
yelling "gee" and "haw" so the horses would turn at the
end of the row.

Catherine was a dutiful daughter, if generally ignored
as her parents hopelessly tried to manage her brother. She
went to Sunday school voluntarily. Her parents were members of the Methodist Church in Livingston but never attended except at Christmas and Easter. She had a good
teacher who had told her to pick the same place to pray
each morning. She couldn't quite manage it. At home in
town she'd go out to a thicket of Russian olive and aspen
trees or, if the weather was too bad, down to her secret place
in the basement where she had an altar covered with her
favorite stones, arrowheads, a pretty white coyote skull, and
her first teddy bear. She loved the Gospels and read them
often and still did. At the farm she'd say her prayers in the
henhouse. She prayed that her parents would stop yelling
at each other and her father would stop drinking so much.
Nothing happened and the teacher said it must be God's

will which puzzled her about the effectiveness of prayers like it does many.

Although she didn't want to, Catherine's mother helped her shovel snow off a big patch of ground outside the henhouse so the chickens could go outside on sunny winter days. Bob the rooster seemed infuriated by his confinement and attacked her mother chasing her across the yard. She was embarrassed to run from a chicken. Catherine rescued her by shouting and waving her arms for Bob who ran back to the comfort of a crowd of hens.

"I'm going to kill that bloody rooster," Mother screamed. Catherine had never heard her mother use that dread word. She had tears of fury in her eyes while Bob was quite happy back annoying the hens.

Catherine had a friend, Laura. They would ride horses together. Laura was slow, or so everyone thought. Then one day when they were feeding the chickens Laura said calmly in a voice different from her usual one that she could actually read and write and that she only acted retarded because it made life easier. Both of her parents were severe alcoholics and were nicer to her under the assumption that she was "out to lunch." Catherine understood because drinking was behind many of her parents' quarrels too. The only one that knew Laura's secret was their cranky family doctor who not oddly approved of her behavior.

The small town had three churches, Lutheran, Catholic, and Methodist. All of the Norwegian farmers and ranchers were Lutherans. If you had a big place it was a ranch, and a smaller one was a farm, often originally part of an early homestead that had been carved up and sold off because it was too much land for a single farmer just trying to get by. It was muttered that the Catholics did well as they had so many children, hence free labor. The Norwegians usually had smaller places and the largest spreads of all were owned by the white Anglo-Saxon Methodists who had moved in with money in banks in the mid-nineteenth century in hopes of getting rich raising cattle. It didn't happen though there had been boom years around the First World War and would be after the Second.

Catherine's brother Robert ran away when he was fifteen and she was nine, still fascinated by her grandparents' chickens. Robert sent a number of postcards from Los Angeles where he said he worked in a Standard Oil station and had started taking drugs. Their father flew out once to look for him but failed. Robert told her years later that he had seen Father from a distance and hid in a car behind the gas station. Father had relentlessly bullied Robert to make him into his own image.

Meanwhile, her parents went through a period when they were sure they had failed as parents and were especially nice to her. They diminished their late afternoon cocktails to a single martini. When they had had several they used to yell at Robert who was brilliant but made poor grades. Their father thought Robert's downfall was his reading. In his early teens Robert had read Dostoyevsky, James Joyce, and many French poets which his father felt had altered his behavior in negative ways. It later occurred to Catherine that if great literature changed your behavior then so what? Their father was unable to see that his bullying led to Robert's rebellious nature. He did not spare the rod. It was also hard on Mother, which was why she would retreat to the farm so often. She was painfully homesick for London, altogether logical since she'd moved to raw Montana on the basis of the lie that she was going to be a farmer's wife. She had a housekeeper named Gert who worked for the family and became a confidante. Later on when Catherine was eleven Gert explained to her that the fundamental problem of her parents' marriage was this lie about the farm. Since childhood her mother had fantasized about being a farmer's wife and perhaps taking the farm over when her husband died. Gert advised Catherine, "A man will tell a hundred lies to get into your pants." Catherine was a late starter and didn't quite understand why a man would want to get in her pants. What would he do there? Soon afterward her mother gave her her first sex lecture which she found stupid and embarrassing. Later on in the spring a boy in the field behind the school took out his hard penis, pointed it at her, and yelled, "Bang." It was the silliest thing she had ever seen, even sillier than Grandpa's pigs screwing, or Bob mounting a hen for a few seconds. Catherine knew that her friend Laura would pick up change from boys for lifting up her dress and showing herself bare. Laura had told her that boys were dumb as male dogs for anything sexual and she needed a little money because her parents never gave her any. They spent every spare penny on drink.

At the farm Catherine would ride on the horse-drawn stone boat, jump off, and gather rocks. Grandpa would stop the team when a rock was too heavy for her and pick it up in his massive hands. Her hands and arms grew strong from the early farmwork so that in the fifth grade when a boy pushed her down she was able to slam him against the wall and choke him. The teacher had to rescue the boy. He warned Catherine about "farm girls" misusing their strength.

One morning in Catherine's eleventh year Mother announced the good news. Her father in London was sending her and Catherine tickets on the *Queen Mary* to visit in England for a year. It was a troublesome time in the world, a scant month before World War II broke out as it turned out, though they didn't expect it when they went. Her father looked happy to see them go. Catherine knew that her father frequently visited a divorcée across town who lived next to Laura's family, which Laura had told her, but her mother didn't know. Of late her mother had been drinking nearly as much as her father which worried her but Catherine thought if she and her mother could just go to the farm, or stay away from town, everything would remain as it was. And she was ecstatic about visiting England on a great boat, said to be the largest in the world that carried passengers.

In early August Catherine said goodbye to her chickens, the only things she regretted leaving behind except her grandparents and Laura. They took a long three-day train journey to New York, stopping for a night in Chicago where her mother had English friends she said were "posh." They certainly were, living in a brownstone downtown near Lake Michigan. Catherine had never seen such furniture and when they arrived from the train station a uniformed man was polishing the doorknob that looked golden though her mother said it was brass. Her mother and the woman of the house were old school friends and laughed a lot. The husband was what was widely known as a "pain in the ass." He had too much to drink at dinner and railed loudly that bankers had gotten a "bum rap" for the Depression. It was obviously a performance for the benefit of a new audience, Catherine's mother Alicia. It became unpleasant though the roast beef was the best she had ever had. The man lurched to his feet before dessert and they heard him crash to the floor with a roar in the den. Servants came running but his wife merely shrugged and smiled and said, "It would be very nice for me if he would break his fucking neck." Catherine's mother and the wife laughed loudly although Catherine worried that the man might be injured.

Breakfast next morning before their noon train was pleasant as the man had long gone off to work.

"You're going to be very lovely. Take care in your choices. You can't be too cautious about who you marry. I'll probably see you in London for a visit," the woman said to Catherine as they said goodbye.

To Catherine the three days in New York City were fine, especially the Museum of Natural History and the Metropolitan Museum of Art. The hard part was her mother's interminable shopping. Catherine wasn't fascinated by clothes the way some girls her age were, in fact she simply didn't care much about them. Her favorite thing to wear was her overalls out on the farm, just like Grandpa's. Her mother, however, had inherited some money from a maiden aunt in Hereford, England. Her father thought that they should buy a new Ford roadster with the money, but her mother had brought the money along in traveler's checks to keep him away from it.

The voyage was utterly grand to Catherine. They had middling tickets, not first class but certainly not steerage. She didn't really know the difference and didn't care. She was completely untraveled and New York City had been stunning in terms of the people she saw. The ship was the same but because it was confined she was able to wander around and study the variety of people as if she were studying her chickens.

The only thing irritating to Catherine was that there was a certain kind of older man who would stare and wink at her. In truth despite her ignorance of sexuality she was a little early in her pubescence and had begun to have breasts. She was five-foot-nine and graceful with big eyes and certain men have a taste for the too young. To Catherine these men were no different from the boy behind the school who had aimed his hard dick at her and yelled, "Bang." She wanted to continue being a girl and had no interest in becoming a woman which she could see was a disadvantage, in Montana and maybe everywhere else. In school even the teachers fawned over the boys who were star athletes. A mere perfect student like herself was largely ignored except by one or two. Luckily her Sunday school teacher Mrs. Semmes had taught her the value of humility which allowed her not to become angry about those conditions she couldn't change. Several years later some girls she knew asked her to join them on the cheerleading squad but frankly she hated the idea of yelling, maybe because of her father who did so much though never at her.

She immediately loved London and her grandparents though she grew quite tired of accompanying her mother on her visits to old friends. Mother treated her as if she were a trophy which she disliked and Catherine was at a loss for anything to say to her mother's schoolmates. Finally she relented and let Catherine take walks with either of her grandparents. They lived about a block off Cheyne Walk in a house that came to them through her grandmother's parents, otherwise it would have been too expensive for them in that lovely neighborhood. They would walk along the Thames and Catherine thought there was no substitute on earth for a big river. London was simply a fabulous walking town and they strayed far in the short time before the war started. It was pretty much all that anyone talked about.

They were there six months when there was a wire saying her mother had to go home because Catherine's grandmother on the farm had died and her father was ill from a possible stroke. Catherine didn't think her mother cared about her father but there were many things to be sorted out that required her at home. She had trouble booking passage as there were so many people trying to get out of England in fear of the possibility of a German attack. Finally Grandfather got her aboard a big yacht returning to Newport, Rhode Island, in exchange for his wangling enough gas for them to reach port. Grandfather had been very high in the civil service, basically looking after all transportation in the London area. Catherine deduced later that this must have been how he wangled gas for the yacht. Her grandfather was called in for many civil defense–type meetings during the war, some at their home during which she had to go up to her room. Secrets were being told and she shouldn't know them. She liked this air of intrigue having read mystery books.

Alicia pretended that she wanted to take Catherine back home with her but Catherine doubted her sincerity. She was still angry about losing her brother and was quite critical as a young woman can be. Catherine's grandmother was dead and her grandfather was ill and she was afraid he'd die and she'd never see him again. Her English grandfather assured her that the Germans would never dare attack "mighty England" as he called it. Then scarcely ten days after they said goodbye to her mother the London Blitz started.

All the nights of the Blitz were spent down in the local subway stop, called the Tube over there. Because of her grandfather's importance he had a little office toward the end of the stop as he needed safe access to a phone. MI5 also gave him two very large guards which consoled her grandmother who lived out the Blitz in a state of relentless fear. They stood right outside the door all night long. Catherine often worried about their families but they had been sent to relatives in the country early on. They were also visited once a day before dinner by grandmother's French cook and his wife Nina. They had a hot plate in the office and Patrice would cook whatever he could scavenge that day from the markets. Grandfather refused to use his importance to get better food than the rest of the city could get because of rationing, but sometimes when Patrice got something particularly good and nondemocratic Grandfather would pretend he hadn't noticed while eating his sacred lamb chop or whatever it was. There was also an open toilet bowl and sink in the office and an electric transformer against the wall which kept them warm on cool nights. They slept with blankets on thin mattresses that would be rolled up and stuffed under the desk during the daytime. So Catherine couldn't complain that her family suffered like thousands of others in the Blitz. At first it embarrassed her to go potty in front of others but when you are hearing the thunder of bombs and the walls are shaking you learn to adapt.

The barrage called the London Blitz continued for fifty-seven nights in a row. Even if you didn't hate Hitler at the beginning you would be insane with rage by the end. Catherine read later that it had killed forty thousand innocent civilians and severely injured about that number. Her birthday fell in October and Patrice managed to make her a cake on the hot plate which made her quite happy, a nice chocolate cake with chocolate frosting.

Catherine felt cheated of the night. She had always loved to walk at twilight and see nightfall, hear the nighthawks and whippoorwills, then stumble home in the dark. Mother would make her take a flashlight but she never used it. The flashlight seemed vulgar in the beauty of the night. She missed most seeing the moon. Grandpa knew this and the evening of the full moon he daringly took her to the top of the stairs to see it. Frederick, one of the guards and a huge Jamaican, escorted them. The moon was distorted by all of the smoke in the air but still beautiful. There were fires all over London from the bombs. They stared at it but suddenly the Luftwaffe dropped the first bombs of the evening not a quarter mile away. Frederick put himself in front of them but Catherine saw the moon turn bright orange from the firestorm. She was both awed and horrified.

Grandpa took her for a walk in the station every afternoon so she could get some exercise. That was when there were the least people in the station. Many left during this time to scavenge for food and to go to the toilet on the streets, as the public toilet in the station was in disrepair. The Red Cross began bringing food which was much appreciated but never enough. Then Patrice was shot trying to steal meat. Nina was bereft but brave and stayed on with Catherine's grandparents until they died. Way into the time of the Blitz one day MI5 sent a small truck that picked up Grandma and Catherine. Grandmother was very ill at the time and the war effort couldn't afford to let Grandfather go with them. The truck, manned by a nice American from Missouri, drove them through the rubble of London. There was a special insignia on the side of the truck and no one tried to stop them. The man from Missouri, named Ted, drove them way out a couple of hours from London to Truro, in Cornwall, to Grandma's brother's small farm. Grandma wept when she saw the farm because she had been raised and given birth to Catherine's mother there. Catherine's heart soared when she saw a big gaggle of chickens in the yard. As soon as she got out of the truck she walked among them crying and speaking soft loving words. A rooster pecked her leg before she could push him away with a foot. It was a solid peck and hurt but she didn't care. Her great-aunt Winifred, called Winnie, made them an early supper because Ted had to drive the truck back to London before nightfall. Catherine would always recall it as the best supper of her life. Great-Aunt Winnie made an enormous omelet with her homemade cheese and served it with a big plate of very red garden to-matoes. Despite what Patrice came up with Catherine hadn't seen an egg in a month and a half because eggs were very precious and she thought she had never tasted anything as utterly delicious in her life. Winnie gave her an Easter basket and it was her job to feed the chickens and gather the eggs as she had done back home in Montana. Most people don't care for chickens, looking at them as food-bearing pests, so everyone was happy when Catherine took over the job. She knew what grand creatures they were and she was pleased to do it. At eighty-five Catherine would still be taking care of her own chickens. When they ate a stewing hen Catherine knew her private name for her. It didn't bother her. It was just part of life.

Chapter 2

Catherine graduated from Barnard in New York City, the female adjunct of Columbia, in 1952. Her mother had a New York apartment (lavish at that) at the same time and relentlessly stuck her nose in Catherine's business whenever possible, which was a problem. She spent an entire winter in New York not calling her mother a single time. Alicia pretended to be bereft.

Mother divorced Father after the war and married the man who owned the yacht that had taken her from England to Newport during the war. Catherine came to suspect it didn't take her mother long to seduce him. She had also discovered another secret about her father aside from his affair with the divorcée, whom she'd seen and didn't think very attractive. Maybe she was nicer to him than her mother, who was rarely acidic with her children but could be merciless toward her husband, particularly when they were drinking. On pleasant summer mornings Father would have his coffee out on a picnic table in the backyard under an oak near the hedge. He always took along his red journal or notebook and didn't want to be disturbed. One morning when Catherine was in her last year at Barnard he rushed off and forgot the journal on the table and she noticed it when she went out to the hedge to check a yellow warbler nest. It was wrong but she couldn't help snooping. To her shock the journal was full of poems he had written. What an unlikely poet this small town banker and bullying father was, she thought. She saw that most of the poems were imitations, not very good, of the English Romantic period of Wordsworth and Shelley but a few terse short ones were fair to good. In general, however, he was too flowery and should read Wallace Stevens, she thought, or William Carlos Williams, a personal favorite of hers.

She wondered how often people had secret obsessions that never saw public daylight. Who acted less "poetic" than her father? Did anyone know besides him? She doubted it. She later read a writer who said, "There must be freedom before there can be freedom." It sounded like nonsense but she thought she understood that we must be ready for our obsessions when they arrive. Like her own interest in chickens. Mother once told her that when she was about two she put her down in the yard while she was hanging wet clothes on the clothesline. She turned to check on Catherine and a hen was sleeping on her lap and she was petting the cozy hen with her tiny hand. She dated this as the beginning of Catherine's chicken obsession but Catherine herself viewed it as far more gradual. And her first move in the barnyard when she first learned to walk was to follow the chickens, getting their poop on her baby shoes. Grandmother tried to stop her but she became distraught so they bought tiny rubber boots they could wash off with the hose. In her eighties she still enjoyed tottering out to feed her hens. They pretended they were interested in her until she threw their food, the scratch, and then they only chased their meal. It was the same when she fed the pigs or calves skim milk, which was left over after the cream when they put milk through the hand-cranked separator. The pigs would watch her approach with eager pig smiles and then she'd pour the skim milk into their trough and they'd be all business. The calves in their pen would mooch up to her like long-lost friends, licking her arms with their rough tongues, and then she'd pour the milk and they'd be at it though not nearly as sloppily as the pigs. Calves would at least look up and around during their meal but not pigs. Compared with both, the chickens were methodical but diffident eaters with more faith apparently in future eating.

Her clue to Father's poetry writing was books. When she and her brother Bobby were quite young her father had given them a set of the twelve-volume *My Book House* saying rather obliquely that books had meant a lot to him as a child. She knew his own childhood library was still in his room in a glass-fronted bookcase so she wondered why he just didn't give them his books, but stayed shy of asking the question guessing there was some kind of emotional involvement as we have for our few precious things.

The twelve volumes of *My Book House* were geared to gradually ascending age beginning with nursery rhymes like

"Pease porridge hot, pease porridge cold, pease porridge in the pot nine days old." Catherine ignored the logic of this progression and read them straight through at age ten, though the late volumes were a little difficult at the time, full of involved folklore and world mythology. The set also fueled her interest in American Indians and one of her own precious things was the small collection of arrowheads and three spear points she had found on the farm. Catherine felt sure reading had fed her father's early interest in poetry. What schizophrenia must have been involved in his later career in economics and banking, but then he had always seemed a man whose character was composed of carefully separated slices. His children and wife never received the tenderness he showed to his English setter bitches Lisa and Clare. Only once had he owned a male bird dog, named Bozo, a rambunctious nitwit who hurled himself over a line of bushes out near the quarry, plummeting downward more than a hundred feet. Father said that only a male dog would jump over something without knowing what was on the other side. After Bozo he owned only females.

But what ultimately carried a man who spent a lifetime writing poetry in secret? We are a mystery. At Barnard and enmeshed in the speedy life of New York Catherine found that around Easter she still believed in the Resurrection as if she could still see the contrail of Jesus rising from death to the heavens. And on spring vacation rather than go to a seaside rental with her wealthy friends she went home to work on her term paper on Kierkegaard and to feed chickens.

❊   ❊   ❊

It was sheer paradise in England to be out of the Tube
station and on a farm. At Grandma's request she'd go next
door nearly a mile and read to a farm couple's son who as
a Francophile had signed up early in the war and lost a
hand and a leg and had his vision impaired in the defense
of Paris. Catherine would read to him for an hour or so and
then have a cup of tea or a glass of beer and chat for a while
with him. He didn't want to hear English classics which
he knew but French and some American novels when she
could find them. Luckily a rich nobleman near the local
village heard about their book plight and gave them access to his library. Her wounded neighbor didn't care for
Hemingway but loved Faulkner's *Light in August* or the
sonorities of *Absalom, Absalom* which made her breathless to
read. The young man Tim was understandably embittered,
a farmer's son who would never be able to effectively farm
himself. One day when his parents were gone he asked to
see Catherine in the nude. She was nearly fourteen at the
time and had been in England for several years now. She
considered his request and thought there was no reason
not to so she quickly stripped but then he started crying.
Later, when he had calmed down with a large whiskey he
tried to explain himself, saying that he felt "dismembered"
and that sexual love was forever out of his range. Catherine
was a young innocent and disagreed saying, "I thought
you just needed that one thing to make love, a penis," and
he laughed at her matter-of-factness. He said that losing
a hand and leg meant that he could never be a *real* farmer,
or a real lover. That was that. She could see that it was a
matter of shame more than anything else.

After the bombings ended Grandma had returned to London to be with Grandfather and the years rolled on slowly with the entire world at war. It was consoling to live on the farm. Her mother would have preferred she come home, but transatlantic travel was now impossible and Catherine was enrolled in a British school and thriving. As an American she was also worried about the Japanese while the local English were obsessed with the possibility of a German invasion. At their dawn breakfast each day her great-uncle Harold, Winnie's husband, was glued to the radio listening to war news. One morning he beamed at her and yelled, "Thank God for the Yanks." The American forces had managed to make a German invasion of England unlikely indeed. Catherine was in love with Winston Churchill's resonant voice whether he was saying something important or not.

One day Catherine got some mail from her grandparents in London who were so pleased to be home and out of the accursed underground. When they had reached home some squatters were in there but it was only a young teacher, his wife, and their baby. Their apartment two blocks away had been utterly destroyed so her grandparents allowed them to make their quarters in a couple of back rooms for the duration of the war. They all liked each other a lot and the young man was skilled enough to replace some windows on the east side of the house that had been broken by the blasts of bombs. The young wife was good in the kitchen, never Grandma's strength, and Grandma loved the little baby boy. Her grandparents were able to visit the farm once in an MI5 vehicle driven by the huge Jamaican, Fred. They ate eggs for three days and returned to London

with several dozen, some cleaned chickens, and a few rab-
bits Harold had raised. The scales finally tipped a bit with
the Normandy invasion but it wasn't until the liberation of
Paris that many people felt any confidence. Catherine heard
later that Hitler had demanded that his officers engineer the
burning of Paris but they had refused to do it. This was a
late in the game relief for her because she had wanted to go
to Paris ever since she had known it existed.

Finally the war was over and it was time for her to go
home. With her parents separated and divorcing there was
no real home for her to go to but she intended all along to
live out on the farm. Still she was reluctant to leave England
and stayed an extra month in London. She liked the young
couple very much and their little boy made her want to have
a baby. She was only sixteen but it seemed logical, if you
wanted a baby, to go ahead and have one. For that reason
she made one more trip after the war out to see Harold and
Winnie. She went directly to Tim's house next door while
his father was haying and his mother was in town grocery
shopping. She took off her clothes in his bedroom, flopped
on the bed bare-assed, and demanded sex. He was utterly
surprised because she hadn't called to say she was coming,
but he didn't seem surprised by her capricious behavior.
He took a condom from the desk and came to the bed with
his crutches. "I've been thinking about this," he said. With
only one hand he couldn't put on the condom by himself so
Catherine hurriedly helped, doing a sloppy job so it would
leak and she might have a baby. His member was large and
she wondered if it would hurt. It did a little but she didn't
care because this was her heart's desire. It was over quickly.

They lay around for a while and then she raised his interest
with her mouth, not something she especially looked forward
to but it worked. She got on him again before he could ask
for a condom.

She didn't get pregnant. She was aggrieved. She was
in tears for a month.

Seventy years later Catherine found it all comically
absurd. She had been willful indeed. She had truly been
a sexual person only periodically. It had been grotesquely
hard in her life to find a good man. Besides, she had never
wanted to be married.

She returned from England on the boat and then a train
to Billings, Montana, and another home. She arrived early
the next morning and Catherine impulsively went straight
to the farm and unloaded all of her luggage. Her grandpa
was still alive, if barely, and she wanted to take care of him
and help him with work. When she arrived he was having an
early afternoon snooze on the couch with the Detroit Tigers
ball game on the radio. He opened one eye and said to her,
"You're home," and went back to sleep. He looked very old
but then she had been gone for five years. In the kitchen
the cook Bertha was cleaning green beans. She looked at
Catherine and smiled broadly.

"You're here! Now I can quit, your grandfather is an
ass."

Catherine merely nodded. She put on her coat and
swiftly walked out.

She made the obligatory drive to town to say hello to
her father. She was dreading it. Mother had said in a letter
that he had been in a bad way since the divorce. She noticed

that the bank was closed early in the afternoon and the shades were drawn but then remembered it was Saturday.

The front door was open at their house and her father sat at the dining room table with a glass and half a quart of gin and his journal in front of him. When he saw her he broke into tears. She didn't remember ever seeing him weep before except tears of rage over her mother or Bobby. It all must have been terribly hard on him, she thought. He had spent his life studying and playing with money and now his wife had run off with a man of ponderous inherited wealth. He had found no way to counter these thoughts except with the emotion of jealousy, gin, and occasional weeping.

"Bobby stopped by while driving someone's car to Chicago. He looked good but wouldn't talk to me. I said you were in England and his mother had left and filed for divorce. He only said, 'Good' and walked out with some of his wretched books."

When she left soon after, the divorcée was coming up the walk with a paper sack, likely another quart of gin. She nodded and Catherine nodded back. At least he had someone but sometimes someone can be less than nothing. A few years later when she discovered her father's poems she thought the better ones were written after her mother left. They were less flowery.

The farm was her home, simply enough. All through high school Catherine helped her grandfather feed and water the cattle and exercise the horses, and the chickens were her special domain. When he saw her off to college Grandpa said to her, "Don't stay too long. This farm is yours now."

After she got home from Barnard, her grandpa was
nearly ninety and facing the prospect of selling his cows
which was a blow to his morale. He couldn't bear the idea
of selling the horses for fear they wouldn't be taken care
of. Occasionally, for reasons of sentiment, Catherine would
help him harness the team of horses and ride the stone boat
while they dragged him through the far pasture. The horses
would automatically stop when they saw a big stone. This
very old man would get off the boat and wrestle the stone
on, to be unloaded later into a pile behind the barn. A friend
of his was the local stonemason and would come out to pick
up a load now and then and he and Grandpa would share
a pint of whiskey.

Later, in the fifties, the farm behind them to the west
came up for sale at $25,000 for 120 acres, a price that Cath-
erine was largely considered a fool for paying at the time,
but she never regretted it. She installed a hired man, Clyde,
and his young wife in the farmhouse on the new acreage.
The wife Clara wept uncontrollably. She had been raised in
a trailer and they now lived in a small trailer down the road
and despaired of ever living in their own house. Catherine
was overwhelmed and had her young lawyer in town cut out
the house and five acres and deed it to Clara personally so
she would stop worrying that her husband could get fired
and she'd be homeless again. Catherine had borrowed the
money from her mother to buy the additional farm and she
had said to consider it a gift, but Catherine intended to pay
it back. Beef prices were fairly high and the pasturage was
good on the new place so she would get a lot more feeders

in the spring. Clara worked for her two days a week and
would bring her little girl Laurel who truly enjoyed the
chickens. She would sit on a milk stool in a daze watching
them with one of the bird dogs, Belle, who belonged to
Catherine's father, sitting beside her. Catherine borrowed
the dog because it didn't look like it was being fed enough,
but told her father that she was thinking of taking up bird
hunting. Grandpa had an old shotgun which her father described as a menace and lent her one of his, a pretty little
English gun she knew was worth a lot so she vowed to be
careful. He wanted to give her lessons but she demurred
for the time being, not wanting to hunt with someone full
of gin. Meanwhile Clara would always make something
for dinner. She was a good cook and after a successful deer
season for her husband she made an old-fashioned venison
mincemeat pie which was delicious.

Chapter 3

Catherine disliked her neighbor who owned a big ranch to the east. It was the early 1960s and her grandfather had died three years before. Running the farm without him was lonely sometimes but she enjoyed it. The neighbor was a lawyer from Dallas and when he drove into her yard he laughed at the chickens she was raising. That embedded him in the mud forever as far as she was concerned. What a motormouth big shot, she thought. When they were raising money for the library he donated a thousand dollars, more by far than anyone else, so Catherine donated two thousand that she couldn't afford just to bust his balls. He had built a pointlessly large house with pillars in front, an imitation of a television program. His wife disliked Montana, and his son and daughter preferred to stay in Texas. His loutish friends and business associates came up to fish for trout and to hunt birds and elk. One of them had paid five thousand

to a relatively poor kid for a giant bull elk to take back to
Texas pretending he had shot it himself. She had once run
into the whole group, the Dallas lawyer and his friends, in
the grocery store buying a case of liquor and whining about
the lack of fine brands. She was wearing a pair of cotton bib
overalls which were admittedly tight across her striking butt.
Out in front in the parking lot when she leaned over to put
her groceries in the car one of the lawyer's friends whistled
and she turned and yelled, "Go to hell, you old creep." The
man blushed and his friends laughed.

In early 1962 she visited her mother in Palm Beach.
It was a monochromatic place. Everyone was rich except
for the legion of mostly black servants. She didn't care for
the place except for her long morning walks. She was thoroughly bored but read a lot, occasionally worrying about her
chickens back home being cared for by Clara. After a few
weeks of this her stepfather, Jerry by name, an odd name for
a rich man she thought, took her fishing in Key West well
to the south. They flew down in a private jet he leased. He
said that flying commercial made him nervous. Her mother
had refused to come along because she had to attend a Red
Cross ball. Jerry had bribed a young man down the street
to take her. Catherine had noted that they had many charity
balls in Palm Beach and she joked that they were planning
a proctology ball. Her mother didn't think it was funny but
Jerry laughed hard. He was a tad silly but saved from his
emotional density by a fine sense of humor. Their fishing
guide, a handsome fellow she thought, picked them up at
the airport and delivered them to a waterfront hotel. Jerry

made much of his claustrophobia and always took a suite. She had an adjoining room and sat at the window for an hour having a margarita and staring out at the ocean. She felt an odd sexual tingle which she attributed to the intensity of the sunlight in the tropics. She thought how chickens needed light to urge them to lay eggs though any kind of light would do. She had made contact with a Barnard friend who was living in Key West with a writer. Jerry had told her that writers came to Key West to misbehave in peace and without criticism. On the way to the hotel Jerry asked the guide to drive them past Hemingway's house which meant little to her. She liked the stories about Michigan and *A Farewell to Arms* but his reputation as a bully and alcoholic reminded her uncomfortably of her father when she learned of it. Young men she had known in college who loved Hemingway had taken absurd steps to act manly. All of which was beyond her own comprehension. Farmers were manly without thinking about it. In fact she had never heard one mention the idea. College itself was so mechanistic that maybe the young men were only seeking a release.

She dozed at the window for a while and then Jerry came in dressed spiffily and said he was having dinner with a friend. She was amused later when walking downtown to a bar to see him on the patio of a restaurant with a hand on the hand of an attractive woman. Evidently deceit was part of being a man. Her friends had a nice little local house, called a conch house, near the Key West cemetery, a charming old place. Her hosts had a party with a half dozen writers from thirty to sixty, very busy drinking and talking about themselves. She had noticed this quality of writers who visited Barnard, the relentless struggle to get the conversation back to them. She never figured out the *why* of this problem. Of course, it wasn't a problem for them, only their listeners.

She liked one of the writers at the party better than the others. He was half French but currently lived in the United States. He wrote mostly about sport, hunting, and fishing, but there was also a novel about growing up in the Normandy countryside that had done well. She was feeling faintly dizzy from too much wine and the thick cigarette smoke in the room. She decided to take a walk and the French writer offered to go with her. This put the others in a snit as she was evidently the prize of the evening.

They walked slowly in the cemetery in the light of the half-moon which made it hard to see and walk without stumbling. It was wonderfully eerie and when she did stumble he caught her and didn't let go. They necked for a while and since her desire had never felt so strong she encouraged him. They tried to make love against a monument to a rich dead man but it didn't work so they ended up with her bent awkwardly over an ordinary gravestone. She tried to read the name upside down while making love but there wasn't quite the light. She lightly traced the engraving with her fingers and came up with "Burke" or "Bruce," probably Bruce. They went on for a fairly long time and she thought it quite wonderful. Afterward they talked a little when they could catch their breath.

"Are you going to put this in a novel?" she asked.

"I don't know. Maybe," he laughed. "I'll call you Mildred not Catherine."

"I don't like Mildred. Make me Italian, call me Lucina."

"Write your own novel," he said seriously.

"I can't. I'm just a farmer. You know, cattle and chickens, a few pigs, wheat and corn, hay."

"That's hard to believe."

"Suit yourself." She went back into the party and was teased a little for her messy hair and crumpled skirt. She wanted to go back to her hotel room.

"That guy you walked with is married."

"I don't care," said Catherine. Then he came in and part of his shirttail was sticking out of his fly. The men laughed. He took her home and they arranged to have dinner the following evening.

She got up very early and Jerry looked bleary and tired but was cheerful. They were running late and after a hasty breakfast they met their guide at the marina. From that point on the fishing day was totally unlike anything she had known or expected. She had thought in terms of rowboats on quiet northern lakes and catching bluegills and perch with her grandfather for dinner. Early on when her father was still trying to make her into a boy he had taken her trout fishing on a big river but it frightened her. She didn't know how to swim yet and feared drowning. If she died, who would feed the chickens? Later on when she had become a good swimmer she swam in the same turbulent river with aplomb, feeling the glory of the rushing current.

That day they fished out of a speedboat-type craft and traveled northwest very quickly to a place Jerry called the "backcountry." They only saw one other boat, a sponger harvesting sponges with a long pole. Jerry had lost his fatigue and was now excited. He told her the ride out here had filled him with "good ole oxygen" as if it were comparable to booze. Jerry cast his big fly rod to several schools of permit but they wouldn't bite. He was nevertheless very happy and Catherine was quite transfixed by the beauty of the turquoise water fading to the brown of sand in the shallows. There were many small mangrove keys breaking up the scenery to the east. They were plainly uninhabited and looked like floating thickets. The two men were looking the other way and Catherine yelled, "Fish!" to alert them as they had taught her. Jerry quickly cast and hooked a big bonefish which they had to chase in the boat so it wouldn't reach a channel and be nailed by a shark. The fish was landed and then released, a lovely act. It was thrilling but not as much as when Mark the guide saw an osprey struggling with a fish it had caught near the mangroves. The fish was too large for the osprey to fly away with it and she feared the bird might drown with its talons stuck in the fish. Mark used his push pole and glided the boat slowly toward the bird. Jerry acted frightened so Catherine made ready to help. Mark put on a pair of gloves but still received a nasty peck in the arm that bled. She managed to hold the bird's wings tight to its body while Mark detached the fish from the talons and threw it into the mangroves. He took over holding the wings and tossed the bird high in the air. It flew off with a backward glare as if they had ruined its meal rather than saving it from drowning. Jerry clapped and laughed which startled her. She felt good that they had managed to save the bird and that she had been a part of it without really knowing how.

It was time to make the long drive back to Key West. First they each had a small rum and Coca-Cola, a drink she'd never cared for but that day it tasted fine and she semi-dozed on the way back.

Chapter 4

That evening they ended up having a room service dinner on the patio of Jerry's suite. Catherine's new friend François joined them and didn't object that they stayed in as she was tired from the sun and heat. They had several drinks including a bottle of good champagne, and she fell asleep in an easy chair after dinner. Jerry and François helped her into her bedroom. She later remembered that Jerry left and François helped her out of her clothes until she was nude, saying, "A wonderful body," and then leaving.

She woke after midnight angry with herself. How was she going to get pregnant if she slept through a splendid love opportunity? She wasn't used to a daylong boat ride in the hot sun. In the morning she called François to apologize and they arranged to meet at the marina when she got back in. François said that he was a friend of the guide and would have him bring them in before five. He would meet her at the marina while she was still awake, he teased, and they could have dinner at his place.

The next day they fished out near Boca Grande Key from which she could see the Marquesas. It looked so lovely in the distance that she wanted to go there but Mark said the channel was too rough today and they would have miles of the choppy water "beating the living shit out of us." Jerry caught a few small tarpon on the edge of the channel, lovely silver acrobatic fish, and then he hooked one that was large. This fish weighed at least a hundred pounds and it jumped half a dozen times with its gill plates rattling, dragging the line in a wide circle with Jerry shouting and his reel screeching. He fought the fish for a half hour and he was soaked with sweat. It traveled south a mile or so out toward the Gulf Stream when Mark suddenly cut the leader when it was close to the boat. He pointed at a very large hammerhead shark coming toward them, drawn into a meal by the struggling tarpon. The tarpon surged off with the hammerhead giving close chase but the tarpon was well ahead in shallow water and the hammerhead turned around. Jerry and Mark were wound up with the fish and chatted about a past experience when they hadn't cut off a tarpon soon enough and a bull shark had made a "bloody mess." All of Catherine's limited fishing experience had been about catching supper. This was something else entirely—the men called it "pure sport" but she wasn't sure. To be pure why not leave the fish alone and just look at it rather than make it fight for its life? she thought, then chided herself for casting judgment. If people wanted to box, let them box and live with their concussions.

François was waiting at the marina and she walked off with him without comment. He had talked with Mark but Jerry kept interrupting with one of his incessant dirty jokes which embarrassed her, not because it was dirty but because he was imbecilic.

She had a good evening and night with François. His rental had a small pool and she immediately shed her clothes and took a dip. François quickly followed with a primitive hard-on. He tried to put his mouth on her underwater but it was awkward. They made love at the shallow end of the pool which was also awkward but more than passable. They made love again on the sofa while waiting for a chicken to roast—butter, garlic, fresh tarragon. She found out that François lived in Palm Beach with a rich wife only two blocks away from Jerry on Sea Breeze Avenue. She said nothing, certainly not that it was the silliest place she had ever seen on earth. All of those rich people jammed together in one place. Why not a farm or ranch?

After dinner and too much fine wine they made love once more desultorily in bed. She fell asleep by ten, utterly fatigued and a little sore all over by the sweet battering. She awoke close after dawn and there were high winds and a tremendous thunderstorm coming in from Cuba, a scant ninety miles to the south of Key West. François drove her to the hotel so she could make a polite appearance for Jerry. He was wandering around in his usual expensive robe talking on the phone. He winked at her and hung up the phone.

"You look rode hard and put away wet," he laughed.

"Some morons say that every day in Montana." Even saying "Montana" made her homesick. What in God's name was she doing in this so-called tropical paradise? She was sick of all things Floridian and wanted to be home feeding her chickens. It was also time to buy a dog not that she was confident she was settled in her life. The only thing that could justify this absurd trip was if she was pregnant. If so there was no way she'd ever tell François. She didn't want a husband or a steady lover, just her farm and chickens, cattle and pigs, a horse or two. She certainly no longer wanted a mother, or father for that matter.

She went into her room to dress and heard Jerry back on the phone and then there was silence. Her door was open a crack and she saw the shadow of Jerry obviously peeking through the crack to see her dress. She poured it on and mooned the door, thinking, what a pathetic fool. She felt a vacuum in her soul where the love of men should have been but the only two she could think of with true fondness were her grandfathers. Had everything gone wrong in the world or was it her? Was it something odd in her strange upbringing that made men uniformly suspect? François was fine but she didn't actually know him very well and there might be something rotten in his heart. She remembered with grief an episode several weeks before when she told the school's young handsome soccer coach to stop by and pick up some eggs. She had thought of seducing him but told him if she was way out back she'd leave two dozen in the mailbox. But she was in the kitchen watching out the window while he wandered around the barnyard and quizzically Sally, a fat hen, was following him. Sally had this irritating practice of pecking at the back of your leg in hopes it would bring food. It was only slightly painful like a quick pinch. Suddenly the soccer coach turned and kicked Sally far in the air. She lay prostrate on her back. Catherine was out of the kitchen in a second, screaming as she came out the back door. The man turned in alarm.

"Why are you kicking my chicken? I think she's dead." She stopped next to Sally and turned her over. The chicken's eyes were sightless. "You killed her you miserable fucker."

"It's just a chicken. I'll pay you for it," he said lamely.

She stood, holding Sally by the feet and slapping the man's face with the chicken. "Get out of here! Now! Go away!" She was sobbing.

He slumped off carrying his presumed innocence like a boy. She was still wild with heart-thumping anger and was glad she wasn't holding a pistol or she would have shot him.

Now in the Key West hotel her stomach soured with homesickness. The weather was clearing and they drove to the airport before noon to catch Jerry's plane home. They met Mark for a quick lunch. She was famished and ate both a grouper sandwich and an order of fresh shrimp while staring east at the ocean.

Back in Palm Beach her mother was happy they were home a day early because there was an "important" ball that evening. Jerry gasped and Catherine only wanted a nap, mostly because she had had a huge Bloody Mary for lunch while Jerry drank two martinis. First she called home and Clyde told her there had been a big snow although it was late April. She was irked because she was missing the fresh snow on the Crazy Mountains east of the farm. She imagined the creamy white mountains in the moonlight.

Who am I and what am I doing? She wasn't used to asking herself such questions. The memory of a depression during her freshman year of college horrified her. The problem, or so she thought, was that New York City had no "outdoors," no snowcapped Crazy Mountains or endless plains. She needed to see a bear that was not in a zoo, or a moose eating water weeds. She escaped this depression by interminable walking, at least four hours a day. She would walk the length of Central Park and back and in every botanical garden in the New York City area. She'd walk along the Hudson and also the East River. When her depression lifted in a couple of months she had lost fifteen pounds she didn't need to lose. Her short and plump Jewish roommate taught her the pleasures of herring and she couldn't get enough. Because she intended to live in Montana she would have to learn how to make her own. The girl also took her downtown to Katz's which immediately became her favorite restaurant in the city.

She had to take a photo of her mother and Jerry before they went to the ball. Her mother, she had to admit, looked lovely in her absurd Pierre Balmain dress. Jerry had all the spark of a dog turd in his tailored tux. He rolled his eyes for the picture which later made Alicia angry when she saw it. She always called him darling which made him beam even if she was angry.

What she had learned about Jerry on their fishing trip raised questions in Catherine's mind about the whole reality of inherited wealth and so did Palm Beach itself. Jerry's father and grandfather had made a great deal of money in the early electronics field. Jerry's father had been a terminal alcoholic and syphilitic giving Jerry zero instruction or guidance in life. His father and grandfather were pure un-adulterated spenders who were so drunk and disorganized that his family freed him of the money and put it in a trust at J.P. Morgan. Only the interest could be spent. Jerry showed good signs early on and graduated from Yale with honors. But then he discovered the ocean which required boats and he ended up with a fleet and many employees in-cluding one who did nothing but help him with his travels. He would go to Europe with twenty pieces of luggage and this required someone to oversee it. He had a great fear of leaving something unspecified behind. He was a grand sucker for luxury hotels. Before Catherine's mother he had had an apartment way up in the Carlyle Hotel because he liked the room service. The expensive secret power it had was to give him lots of bacon on his order.

Jerry was an expert in the fields of anthropology and ornithology. No place was too far to go see a bird. In his Rhode Island house he kept drawers full of thousands of dead birds, bought from a European collector and smuggled in on the yacht including a unique specimen that he shared with no one but willed to Harvard on his death. What's the hurry? he thought. A few years before Catherine's mother showed up he had been married to a French actress for a scant five months. He had taken her down to Cannes to the movie festival and this seemed to make her less popular. He had been married a total of four times and his ironclad rule was no children. He considered himself to have greatly suffered in childhood and would wish it on no one else. His family fortune was aimed at a not very significant college in Ohio. On one of his early, random cross-country drives he had stopped in the college town for the night and liked its aura and the fresh, hardworking people. The college as of yet didn't know he existed and he didn't realize that his money would destroy the charm of the place. He was almost a nitwit but not quite.

Chapter 5

Catherine left Palm Beach several days later and didn't get home until midmorning a day late. The plane had had a long delay in Denver with a driving rain that turned into driving snow. She got to Billings late, picked up her car, and drove up to Roundup because she wanted to head home on Route 212 which to her was the ultimate Montana road because it reminded her of the old Montana of her childhood before so many rich people moved west. "All hat and no cows," as people said. She stayed in a scummy little motel where perhaps drunk truckers had pissed on the rug. She was famished having skipped the loathsome airline snacks. There was an open bar and she hoped for a single hamburger. It turned out that they had passable small rib steaks of which she wolfed two. Two polite cowboys at the bar made equally polite passes at her. "If you don't got a place to stay I have a clean bunkhouse." She danced with one who smelled slightly of manure and horses but not offensively. She could really cut a rug but held back from showing off. As a senior at Barnard she had a little apartment down in the Village with a Puerto Rican girl Josita who loved dancing. They danced together insatiably with Josita in drag. They won a number of dance contests with the judges perceiving that Josita was also a woman—her ass was too shapely to be male. One night when drunk they slept together but Catherine didn't care for it. As stupid looking as they were she still preferred dicks.

She couldn't hold back and the cowboy was breathing hard. There was applause and then drinks from a table of old ranchers. They slow danced to Patsy Cline singing "Crazy" and he blushed deeply.

She bought a pint and went to her motel, pouring a big one because she was still jangled from Florida. In bed watching the late news she recalled there was one other man she actually liked aside from her grandfathers. That was wounded Tim who lived next door to Great-Uncle Harold and Great-Aunt Winnie just near the Cornwall border. Her grandmother had written that he was finally making some progress with prosthetic devices which he had refused to try for a couple of years but then his goofy grandmother had taken to praying on their stone driveway on her knees in all weather so he caved in. He could now shuffle along passably with his big walking stick and when he fell he was strong enough to shimmy up the stick with his good hand and the artificial one. Anyway he was the third man she admired and she very much wanted to make love to him and hopefully become pregnant. She was past thirty and felt time slipping away. He was so bitter about the severity of his injuries she doubted he would ever let her close.

She awoke early and figured out the room coffeepot. She felt slow-witted and wondered if she was losing her mind, a concept she had always disagreed with. How could you *lose* your mind? It was always there though it could be in severe disrepair. She felt mired in random thoughts such as realizing she shouldn't have fired the lawyer who when working on her will had laughed when she insisted her cremated ashes should be strewn on the floor of the chicken coop.

Part II

Chapter 6

When she got home and took in her luggage there was a note stuck on the door from her father which she put off reading because she was moving her camping cot out to the chicken coop. She meant to spend her first night home in the company of her beloved chickens, a somewhat eccentric means of returning to normal.

She read her father's note with a luncheon tuna fish sandwich mostly because he hated tuna. The note was a shock and written on Best Western stationery because he was staying there until he found a place. Her brother Robert had stopped for a visit while hitchhiking from Los Angeles to New York City. The visit was "highly wretched" and "insulting." Robert warned him that he was going to burn the house down. "I said but you left a whole room of your precious books here. That seemed to give him pause so I didn't call the police about it. We drank a whole bottle of

gin together and things further degenerated. That night
he did burn the house right to the ground. I barely got out
alive but was awakened by the heavy odor of gasoline. I got
both dogs out but lost my precious collection of shotguns
and antique maps. The police found Robert asleep in a ditch
about ten miles east of town. He is now incarcerated in the
county jail. I asked the prosecutor to press all charges. He
should be locked up for life. Sad to say this grand home
would have been yours when I am deceased."

She called the jail in the county seat about twenty miles
distant in Livingston. Yes, she could visit Robert until five
that afternoon. She had actually always disliked the house.
It had been owned by a minor railroad baron. There's nothing new, she thought, about "conspicuous consumption,"
as Thorstein Veblen called it. Her friends thought it was
haunted. It was dour, gloomy, and even smelled ancient.
When young she had found a small secret room in the basement which was a fine place to hide her pathetic secret
belongings though no one was looking.

Her night on the cot in the chicken coop was very pleasant. Of course it smelled of chickens and chicken shit but
she was used to that and had missed it. She brought out a
book to read but didn't touch it. She just wanted to be in
the dark hearing the soft murmur of clucking hens. Were it
not for the beauty of the ocean and the fishing she certainly
wouldn't think of Florida again. She had long been curious
about France and also Mexico. If she went to France she
could stop in London and see her grandparents, also drive up
to see Harold and Winnie and of course Tim. But for now it
was so nice to be home she doubted she'd want to leave again.

She petted a couple of chickens that came close out of curiosity about their guest. She dropped off into the deepest of sleep and when she woke at dawn two were roosting down by her feet on the cot. She was utterly charmed and laughed at which point they stared at her. It was so pleasant to be totally accepted by other creatures. Once she had met a man who had raised an Alaskan brown bear since infancy. Even when the bear was in its late teens it still had to be hugged at least twice a day. It had died recently at the weight of fifteen hundred pounds. She had a photo on her bulletin board of them hugging, the bear's massive head at least five times the size of the man's. The bear seemed to be smiling. She went inside and prepared to drive to Livingston to see Robert. There was a note from Clara, a message from the family doctor that her father was in the hospital and was quite ill. She called in and discovered he had had another stroke and was not expected to survive. She felt a bit of relief as his life depressed her. He did nothing but walk his dogs a short distance and drink a quart of gin every day. He was kind to her now but they had no real conversations. She called her mother in Palm Beach who said she was not coming back to Montana at "gunpoint" to see her dead ex-husband.

"He's not dead yet," Catherine said.

"He is to me," she said, hanging up. She called back immediately. "I'm so sorry but it's been wonderful being rid of that pompous wanker. It was only good when you and I were out on the farm without him. Meanwhile I want to go to France and Jerry doesn't want to. Will you go with me? It would be free for you."

"I'll think about it. I have a farm to run." Catherine had always wanted to go to Paris but her first impulse was that traveling there with her mother would be insufferable. Catherine didn't want to go but then she didn't have much in the way of spare money. The money her father should have left her had all been spent or drunk away.

Chapter 7

The trip to see Robert in jail didn't go well. It was a forlorn and ugly place. She was escorted by a deputy and when the prisoners made smutty remarks as they passed he would smack on their bars with a nightstick. She sat on a folding chair and watched Robert doze on his cot. He awoke slowly glancing at her as if in disbelief.

"When you get out of jail you're welcome out at the farm," she said.

"You're the farmer not me. I'm a city-billy."

"I got you a good lawyer."

"Don't bother. I already saw the jerk. Don't spend your money. I'll get a public defender."

"They're talking about a three-to-five-year sentence."

"I'll commit suicide before I go to prison." He didn't seem unhappy announcing this.

"Don't say that Bobby."

"It's true. It seems like we were okay until all of that yelling and boozing started."

"Our father is on his deathbed right now."

"Good. It's too bad he didn't die when we were kids. What an asshole. I'm sorry I burned your house down."

"I don't care. I never liked that house. I think my marble collection is still in my room in the basement."

"They might be okay. I don't think marbles burn. I want to go to South America."

"Why?"

"I want to go to the pampas where there are no people and kick this drug thing. Maybe chase cows on horseback."

"I'll loan you the fare," she said, her heart wrung with despair. He seemed small and pathetic in the jail cell. "You burned up your books in the house. That's too bad."

"I don't want to read anymore. I'm going to write a book called *O Mein Papa*." He laughed.

When she left the jail she wanted to vomit over what fathers and mothers did to their children. How had she escaped? Her chickens helped.

Chapter 8

One afternoon a few months later she got home and heard a cow bellowing in distress in the far pasture near the woodlot. She trotted way out there as quickly as possible noting near the horse trough that all that was left of her precious dead hen was a clump of feathers. A present to the ubiquitous coyotes. She made a mental note to call about getting an Airedale from a farmer who raised them. A big male would keep the coyotes out of the barnyard before they got bold enough to start picking off chickens in the daylight.

She reached the bellowing cow along the creek and saw that her calf was stuck in the mud in an eddy of the creek and on the verge of drowning. She jumped in without a thought and wrestled the little calf up onto the bank. The calf licked her face then started nursing from its mother who had trotted over. Catherine had trouble getting out of the mud herself and lost a tennis shoe. She walked all the way home with one foot bare and quite sore by the time she reached the pump house attached to the back door. She remembered that early every summer it took a few weeks for bare feet to toughen up before they were comfortable, and she supposed she was getting an early start.

She impulsively called an ob-gyn doctor she knew quite well in Livingston. She kept thinking about pregnancy but maybe she was fallow and incapable of being a mother. Was this why it hadn't worked before? There was a cancellation early the next morning and she promised to be there. If she could be fertile all she needed was the right man or at least an acceptable man. She knew above all else it was wounded Tim over in Cornwall but then his sensitivities prevented him from being counted on. They corresponded now and then in letters that were decidedly nonromantic. He felt good that he had lost his left hand rather than his right so he could still write a letter. He never mentioned that he was using the prosthetic devices that her grandmother had spoken of in her note. When she made the mistake of mentioning Tim to her father once, he judged that losing a limb would always be an embarrassment. He said that it "unmanned" him. This concept missed her as a woman but then so-called male pride had been one of her father's most obnoxious shortcomings.

She had a difficult night full of baby dreams and woke asking herself was she daft? Something in her answered no. It was an inexplicable urge. At the doctor's office she was roundly teased by her ob-gyn friend for bringing her a dozen eggs. She explained that she wanted a baby but no husband. She could afford it.

"What if it's a little boy who needs a daddy to teach him baseball?"

"I can play baseball. I'll teach him." In fact Catherine was a good athlete. "I can also teach him to hunt."

"Have you chosen your rooster yet?"

"No, that's the problem. Finding a father."

"So I noticed." Liz the obstetrician was perpetually in search of a new man in her life. She was more than a bit stocky which didn't seem to help. She kept a fireman and a carpenter on a sexual string by cooking grand meals for them. She knew very well that dieting might help but she was a fine cook and looked at food as the only compensation for her wretched life far from her homeland of Chicago. The town was a bit scandalized by her behavior but she was the best obstetrician around, and one of the few women in the field in the entire country.

Catherine had gone on a three-day trip to Chicago with her the year before. It was hard to wedge in everything that needed eating from delicatessen food to outsize rib steaks. Catherine had to pass on the last dinner and it was a full week at home before she had fully recovered. That last evening alone had been lovely. It was April and stayed light fairly late. They had a small suite at the Drake and she could see wondrous Lake Michigan out three different windows. She had always meant to drive around it. She merely sat in an easy chair gazing at it until she slept.

They sat and chatted, Liz explaining the technical aspects of conception from zygote to blastocyst. When the doctor mentioned eggs Catherine was visibly startled.

"What's wrong?"

"I haven't thought consciously about my eggs since high school." It unnerved Catherine to know that the eggs she hadn't appreciated might now prevent her from having a baby.

They laughed but Catherine felt a nonspecific unrest that continued as she drove home. Before she went into the house she fed the chickens a goodly amount of late afternoon scratch. She didn't want to think about eggs so she naturally thought about eggs. She thought about eggs through a long sleepless night. At 5:00 a.m. she poured herself a big clear glass of wine and sat by the window and waited for the reassurance of dawn. Her father's doctor called as early as was permissible to say her father had died in the night. She felt nothing. The death didn't stop her from thinking about eggs and she was beginning to feel cursed so she took a very long walk at dawn. At the far end of the west pasture there was a good-size rock pile that reminded her of a heap of eggs from a distance. Eggs again. She thought of riding on the stone boat behind Grandpa's team gathering rocks years before.

On her way back to the house she admonished herself for this silliness about eggs. That helped as recognizing absurdity lightens its load. She pondered the brutal simplicity of the human body, at the same time its intricacy. Liz had said that her only religious feelings came directly from her work. How could it all be an accident? Catherine couldn't relate. She had prayed back during the Blitz that a bomb wouldn't land on her head and it hadn't. It seemed fair to pray for others but not yourself. She had prayed back in Sunday school that her father wouldn't hit Robert but that prayer hadn't been answered. She had so dreaded his funeral that she was tempted to call the funeral home to say she was ill and couldn't attend. No one would be there except the divorcée and a few old hunting friends, she had thought. Then she remembered that it was the opener for trout fishing and the weather was fair so those men would likely be fishing. It saddened her that her father had had so few people to draw around him.

She was having a rough day and napped for a half hour after her long walk. Unfortunately a nightmare came with the long nap. She was in a great marble hall and the floor was covered with eggs. The floor was tilted slightly and the eggs were rolling slowly and gently toward an altar she must reach. She stepped on a few and the crackle under her feet was repulsive to her in her sleep. She slipped and fell and broke a dozen more.

She awoke in a sweat and quickly dismissed the idea of making an egg salad sandwich for lunch. Farm people were forever trying to use up their extra eggs, even in their potato salad, but not today. She drew a chuck patty from the freezer and also a rib steak to thaw for dinner. The beef came from a prime steer they had butchered last December. The meat was wonderful and she split it with Clyde and his wife and children who were thrilled. Truly fine beef is out of nearly everyone's range. Her butcher had space to hang the carcass for forty days which increases flavor and all the shrinkage is only water. She was still full of agita about eggs which gave rise to the idea of getting a hysterectomy and living and dying childless. Instead she called her travel agent and booked a plane passage to England for March, to see her putative lover. He certainly didn't think of himself that way.

She was getting forgetful as if she were far older than she was. She had reserved a puppy and then neglected to pick it up at the owner's. She knew she should have waited until she got home from England to get the pup but she also knew the owner wouldn't tolerate further delay. She had read altogether too much on the subject of puppy raising and she knew she should be present for the first few weeks to properly imprint it but then she wanted a dog not a science project. She would have accepted her father's Belle but he had left the dog to a sporting friend.

When she got to the dog owner's house the pups were in a small pole barn to protect them from rain. The mother wagged her tail in friendly greeting but Catherine's choice, a male, rushed out as if to tear them apart. He was defending his two little sisters, or so he thought, against humans. The man picked him up and gave him a little shake, then held him for a minute. He handed the dog to Catherine and he growled lightly then flopped back in her arms and closed his eyes, another male sucker for a hugging.

"I've been calling him Hudley or Hud. You know, after the movie when Melvyn Douglas says to his son Paul Newman, 'Hud, you're no damn good.' Of course now he's your dog so you can call him what you like."

"I think Hud is a good name," she said. She was a little embarrassed because the dog was getting a tiny erection.

"He never does that with me," the man laughed. "It's interspecies love."

Hud resisted being put in the crate for the ride home and wailed when they were in motion. About a mile down the gravel road she pulled over and let him out. He scrambled into the front seat and glared as if to say, "This is where I belong." She could already see he wasn't going to be easy though he sat on the front seat like a gentleman, short of snarling at some cows they passed. At home she fed the chickens which he ignored. The owner had had chickens and said that he had been trained to leave them alone. The exception was that the rooster strutted up and pecked him in the ass. This meant war. Hud growled and attacked. The rooster escaped by flying over the fence and landed at the edge of the water trough. She grabbed the pup, swatted him on the ass, and said, "No" loudly. He lay in the dirt obviously feeling wronged. She took him to the pump shed attached to the back door of the house which she had planned as his quarters. There were several old blankets and pillows arranged in a corner. She fed him a large bowl of puppy chow which he wolfed then arranged him on his bed. He promptly went to sleep as if he had done a long day's work.

She made her own dinner of fried breaded pork steak with cayenne and garlic in the flour. It was a distinctly lower-class dish which she had always loved. She also made broccoli in penance but did it Oriental style which made it nearly edible. Later that evening she was rereading some Evan S. Connell when Hudley starting howling on the back porch. She went out and said, "No" and slammed the door. Soon enough he resumed his howling and she called the owner in desperation. He admitted that all the pups had regularly slept on his daughter's bed. "You're going to have to gut it out," the owner insisted, and he would finally learn to sleep alone. The owner put Catherine on the line with his daughter which led to nothing. The daughter finally said, "What's wrong with Hud sleeping with you? You aren't married, are you? He wants companionship. Don't you?" Catherine let that one pass. The pup howled intermittently until midnight when Catherine quit reading and decided on bed. Tomorrow she would take Hud on a very long walk and tire him out. She would exhaust him and then he would sleep normally.

The minute she got into bed he started the worst howling yet. She figured he had seen the crack of light under the door of the dining room go out. She lasted only about ten minutes until she went out and got him and plopped him on the bed. He had an air of victory and she thought you asshole. It might be difficult to have a male houseguest. He snuggled up against her chest uncomfortably like a baby. He was immediately asleep and in the morning was in the same place snoring softly. She eased out of bed and he quickly followed her into the kitchen. She made herself two boiled eggs and cracked two for Hud which she mixed with his puppy chow to give him a shiny coat, as the puppy book encouraged. He ate his breakfast in seconds and slumped down in the blankets of the pump house and fell back asleep. Evidently the place was good enough for naps. She tiptoed out and went to the kitchen table and read poetry for half an hour, a long-held morning habit. She was currently reading an anthology of Chinese poetry. She had long loved Chinese poetry because it soothed her in a way other poetry didn't. For instance Auden but especially Wallace Stevens could

trouble her. Read them in the morning and then you had to
carry the puzzle with you all day.

Her good intentions double-crossed her again. She
walked Hud on a long circular route out through the pasture.
She estimated she had walked him five miles in two hours
before he collapsed on the ground. It took a few minutes
for her to figure out that he wanted to be carried which was
awkward though they made it to the rock pile for a rest.
He saw a black snake and he was immediately enraged,
pursuing the snake until it disappeared within the rocks.
She yelled, "No." There were no rattlers on the farm but
enough in the rock cliffs two miles behind it that she wanted
to discourage any interest he had in snakes. Many people
had lost small dogs to rattlers though a big dog could usually
withstand the bite of a western diamondback. Her father
had always carried a small .22 pistol loaded with magnum
BB shot to plug them in the head but then she didn't want
to kill anything. It made more sense to train the dog to keep
away from them. He ignored the cows, probably thinking
that they were too large to be understood. It was quite funny
when curious cows followed him until he was batty with
anger. The cow and puppy were nose to nose with the cow
ignoring the snarls with no idea that she might be under
attack from a thirty-pound puppy.

They were still a mile from home when Hud nestled
in the grass demanding to be carried. He truly was still a
baby, she thought, picking him up in her arms. When she
reached the water trough she dropped him in because he
was soiled from rolling in the dirt and manure in the pasture.
He was furious paddling around growling. When she lifted

him out and put him down he ran into the barnyard and
rolled in dirt and chicken shit until he was suitably soiled
and smelled interesting on his own terms. She knew that
a daffy woman in the county seat had an obedience school
for dogs and it was obvious that Hud should be enrolled.
She got him in the pump house and washed him off with
two wet, hot washcloths telling him, as he growled out of
dislike for being washed, that if he was going to sleep with
her like any male he couldn't be a stinker. When she was
little her brother Robert screamed and cried when Mother
washed his hair. Now Robert was doing three to five in the
Deer Lodge prison. She had gotten him a good lawyer but
he had been impertinent and insulting to the judge, not a
good idea. She remembered with amusement the story of
an old cowboy down the road who had been arrested for
drunk and disorderly yelling at the judge, "Kiss my ass you
bald-headed son of a bitch. Come down off that bench and
I'll kick your ass all over the courtroom." He did extra time
but was much admired by the many louts in the area.

Hud slept off his hike and Catherine made a beef stew
with a lard crust. Her grandmother had taught her the crust
for stews, pie, and her signature chicken potpie which Catherine hadn't quite mastered and often craved. The only ones
that had come close were in Jewish delicatessens in New
York City. She would treat herself to one when she had the
New York City blues from too little sunlight and too many
people. Another option when she was feeling lethargic was
to take the subway with her Jewish roommate down to
Houston Street and go to Russ and Daughters for half a
dozen pieces of herring then walk awhile, then down the

street to Katz's for a monster corned beef, tongue, or pastrami sandwich. Compared with Katz's they simply didn't know how to make a sandwich in Montana.

A month later she had her hired man Clyde come in the kitchen for a meeting. He was nervous and fretful so she put his mind at ease explaining that she had to go to England so it would be better if he stayed in the house rather than his wife since she now had Hud who could be unmanageable. He had been a champ in his obedience classes but saw no application of what he learned there to his life at home. He had killed a woodchuck out by the barn and hidden it in a very thick grove of lilacs in front of the house. She had tried to crawl in to get the woodchuck away from him but failed. The woodchuck stank and Hud seemed prepared to run with his prize. Right now she was irked at the way Hud was fawning over Clyde's leg as if he were a long-lost cousin. It was an absurd case of male bonding. Clyde said that he would be glad to stay here and look after Hud and then they took off for a stroll around the barnyard.

Catherine took a hasty shower and noted in the bedroom's full-length mirror that she was becoming a little thin. That wouldn't do because she knew Tim didn't like skinny women. It was a week before her departure and she vowed to load up on fatty pasta recipes. When she saw a pregnant woman at the grocery she was shot full of jealousy. She came home and put a pork shoulder in a pot of marinara sauce with lots of garlic to slow cook so that the meat and fat would soften making a wonderful pungent sauce for rigatoni. She had learned the recipe from a rather tubby red-haired Italian in New York who worked as a chef. He was an energetic lover but she had to ditch him because he drank too much and she had the horrid memory of her parents. She stuck to modest amounts of wine herself, white in the summer and red when the weather cooled. She naturally worried about addiction. Look at her miserable brother and drugs. He had merely stepped across the abyss of his parents' alcoholism to narcotics.

Chapter 9

When she landed at Heathrow via Chicago her grandfather was waiting with the same big Jamaican driver from his job. She was tired but quite happy. On the way to his home they stopped at the Tube station where she had spent the Blitz so she could take a look. All the memories depressed her though she was now over thirty and that had been when she was twelve. A memory returned of a man holding a knife to her and making her blow him in a dark corner one day while the night guards were off duty and her grandparents were away. She gagged on his penis then vomited after he ejaculated. She had told no one and tried to repress the memory, not wanting to cause more trouble than they already had. Now when she saw the dark corner again she felt cold sweat rising to the skin of her forehead.

She had a pleasant five days with her grandparents who looked awfully old and she promised to stop back after she

visited Harold, Winnie, and Tim. Her grandmother understood but her grandfather worried that she would break her
heart over the amputee. She rented a car and drove out to
Cornwall with no difficulty on a beautiful sunny day. Grandmother had made her a brisket sandwich with horseradish,
one of her favorites, and she pulled off on a side road and ate
while staring at a field of just-sprouted oats on the side of the
road and horses on the other including some rambunctious
fillies to whom her stopping was an important event. They
ran up to the stone fence and she touched their little noses
and warm necks. She was thrilled to the point of shivering. She had talked on the phone to Clyde who had had no
trouble with Hud. His behavior had been perfect except he
had killed the rooster after it pecked at his face. The rooster
was an asshole like all his predecessors so Catherine didn't
really care. She would get another one when she needed
chicks. Hud had run into the lilac thicket with his kill but
Clyde had retrieved the rooster and stewed it. He told her
that while he was growing up in a big poor family his father
had a connection for cheap roosters, and as a little boy he'd
learned to pluck them. They were a tad gamier than hens but
certainly edible, especially stewed with biscuits on the side.

She spent a couple of days at Harold and Winnie's, all
the while staring at Tim's place a mile down the road. She
had confided in Winnie who was sympathetic. "The point
is if you can afford a baby," Winnie had said. "Why have a
husband when they love to act like they don't have wives
when they're away?" She finally called Tim early the next
morning. He hadn't answered her last two letters but she
knew it was hard for him. The phone rang six times before

he picked up and she thought of him shuffling to answer it on crutches. He sounded melancholy indeed but said this was a good day to visit because his parents would be away for their annual quarrel with the tax assessor.

She put on a short skirt in hopes of sexually intriguing him but then it seemed too obvious and in the end she went for a skirt that was a little longer. It was nearly a half hour walk. Her feet got wet and she had to wind her way through two thick hedges and crawl over an awkward stone wall. Their sheepdog came out halfway and happily greeted her after a single bark. He bore a striking resemblance to the dog years before who thought he was Tim's guardian. All the way on her walk she became more and more angry about the irrationality of war. The more than eight hundred thousand casualties at Verdun. A whole generation of young French had passed on and England also came close to losing a generation. She had grown up in the shadow of the two world wars and she sometimes could not bear to read the poets. "I have a rendezvous with death" indeed. Millions died.

Tim was shy and withdrawn at first as she sat on a swing on the back porch. His arm stump fitted in a slot on the crutches and one of his legs was pegged. She sat facing him listening to the chattering birds and sipping coffee and trying to use her bare legs to advantage. He relented and they made their way into his bedroom. In the next six days they made love a couple of times a day. His parents at first pretended not to notice her presence and then welcomed her warmly. On her last day he looked at her oddly.

"You look a little smug."

"I'm trying to get pregnant by you." And then she con-
firmed everything.

"But why me? Find yourself a husband."

"I don't want a husband except you. I just want a baby
to raise."

He was overwhelmed and began weeping, and barely ut-
tered, "I don't want you to spend your life taking care of me."

"But why, if I love you? I want to marry you this afternoon." Her voice quivered never having said "I love you"
before.

"Everybody's sympathy wears out," he choked.

She kissed him and walked home where she had a stiff
drink of Harold's whiskey. God damn the world and its wars,
she thought. Those who start the wars never die in them. She
packed hastily, had supper with Winnie and Harold, read,
and went to sleep, getting up early for the drive to London.
Winnie got up and made her breakfast and a sandwich for
the trip. Country people everywhere were suspicious of
restaurants with many stories of a fly in the soup.

When she reached London her grandmother was off
shopping for dinner and her grandfather looked at her quizzically, saying, "You look blue." It came out in a rush from
her sexual abuse in the subway to Tim's refusal to marry her.
Her grandfather did the best he could to soothe her. Way
back then her abuser had been a braggart and Frederick the
Jamaican found out and had pushed the man in front of a
train. She was stunned, wondering if the man deserved to
die for his sins. She was not a vindictive person but maybe
it would save other girls. She and Frederick agreed not to
tell anyone else. About Tim her grandfather said, "One of

the ironies of war is that it makes the severely wounded feel worthless. There is no reward for them."

Catherine took a long walk. There was still stray rubble here and there from the Blitz but in general the city was in good shape. She loved walking along the Thames, however dirty. She noted that many of the mansions along Cheyne Walk had been totally reconditioned by the magic of lots of money. She chided herself for her hopeless guilt about war and history and being a woman not called to help or protect Tim in battle. Now they could have nothing.

Chapter 10

Catherine was home on the farm for a month before the momentous discovery that she was pregnant. She danced and shrieked in the obstetrician's office. The doctor was amazed and happy for Catherine.

At home although it was a cool day she danced herself into a sweat while feeding the chickens. Hud ran around barking and snapping at her heels. He clearly disapproved of this behavior that had nothing to do with him. Dogs prefer that we behave the same way every day. If we don't, maybe we'll forget to feed them! Even the hens scattered in alarm. She had to acknowledge it was pleasanter without the rooster.

When finished with her dancing Catherine knelt and comforted Hud and then threw the hens extra scratch for putting up with her. She took Hud for a little walk about a hundred yards behind the barn to a small pond and a bone pit where her grandfather had dragged the carcasses of dead animals, cows and pigs. Hud loved the pile of ancient bleached bones still with their scent of meat. He had also eaten a muskrat from the pond. Catherine couldn't catch him and he wasn't about to give up a trophy merely because she said, "Drop it."

She had some worries about pregnancy and child care despite the stack of books she had accumulated. It was easy to recall that books and classes hadn't helped with Hud. He would heel when they walked the gravel road and a vehicle was coming but then there was a real urgency in her voice. He greeted "come, sit, stay" with a yawn. Dogs are good judges of intention in the voice. Also he had a terrier's bad temper and sometimes a "come" would cause him to glare at her and back into the shrubbery. Yelling didn't help. It seemed to him to mean that he had won the round. He was a free radical, pure and simple. He was wildly appreciative when she returned from the store or wherever as if he might have been abandoned. The most effective command was "cheese" because he loved a piece of cheddar.

The idea of eggs had followed her ever since her second-grade report on chickens and not always pleasantly. Eggs were the fundamental fact among all females in the mammalian and most other species. One of hers was currently fertilized for better or worse though it was what her heart wanted. Her old school friend Laura now had three children. She had once admitted in high school to Catherine that her cousins were always screwing her. But she was rather homely and was still faking mental problems so the high school boys ignored her. The point was that cousins were better than nothing, or so she said. This appalled Catherine who was a virgin at the time. When she even touched a boy's penis he was always shooting all over the front seat and making a mess. Laura seemed to have turned out okay, or perhaps Catherine just wanted the children her friend and her husband had, seemingly without effort.

Catherine had figured out early on that people were primitive right below the surface. She remembered Gert telling her at eleven, *A man will tell any kind of lie to make love to you*. She couldn't quite figure out her mother. When Catherine was a little girl they would drive out to the farm singing songs all the way. They were truly happy which made the decline more upsetting when her mother began drinking right along with her father in the late afternoons and early evenings. While Catherine was living in England Winnie told her how happy her mother had been when they became engaged. She would finally move from crowded London to an actual farm. Winnie said Alicia had spent most of every summer with her and Harold and worked like a man. She was born to be a farm girl and when she found out that he was lying the disappointment was fatal. And now she was in Palm Beach and Oyster Bay, the least farmlike places imaginable except the heart of Calcutta. The message to Catherine had been to go it alone as much as possible. Jerry's lavish gifts had been very helpful but he didn't know how helpful they were. Once when passing through by chartered jet, for he refused to fly commercial except to Europe, Jerry had stopped by for lunch and suggested to Catherine that he try to buy out her blowhard

Texas neighbor. She asked him to wait as she wasn't sure she could run such a large ranch.

Catherine took Hud for a little walk to shake off her dark mood and was amused when he hopelessly chased a jackrabbit that was much faster than he was. He finally slumped to the ground and looked like he was feeling sorry for himself after his failed game of catch, kill, and eat. It seemed that her life was accelerating in a direction she had chosen but at a speed she couldn't quite emotionally encompass. Her mind felt quivery but tentatively sane. It reminded her of her junior year in college when she thought she was going nuts. Since she passably read Spanish she had agreed for a poetry class to write an essay on Lorca's *Poet in New York* which was still fairly new at the time, maybe ten years since its publication shortly after the poet's murder which had dumbfounded her. The project was unwise as the book drove her batty. She had loved Lorca's *Gypsy Ballads* but had in error assumed this was the same kind of book, far indeed from the truth of the matter. What was a girl from Montana to make of a section named "Landscape of a Vomiting Multitude"? She tried to back out of the essay but the professor wouldn't allow it because he was interested in what she had to say about the surrealism of the book. He was in his late sixties but was obviously sweet on her and said she must write the paper as he was curious about what she thought. In his office she sat in a low easy chair which she figured he had in order to look up the legs of girls, so she showed a lot of leg to tease the wicked old lecher.

What saved her on this project whose horrors had been exacerbated was the essay on *duende* that Lorca had written,

which her professor encouraged her to read alongside. The
essay made clear for the first time why she loved the kind of
music and poetry she did. The art she loved had *cante jondo*, a
ghostliness that drew out one's most deep-seated emotions. It
didn't matter if it was Beethoven or Carlos Montoya simply
playing the guitar which at one point had made her sob. Stan
Getz would later touch her the same way. Perhaps it was
strange in retrospect how utterly infatuated she had become
with the poet after reading *Gypsy Ballads*. She had fantasies
of making love to him on the bank of a river in Andalucía,
then she discovered that he had been born gay and now was
dead at the murderous hands of Franco's men in Granada.
She felt foolish for her heartbreak but then there are no
limits to the emotional life.

Chapter 11

Her pregnancy was difficult. She had interminable bouts of morning sickness and after two months there was a horrifying letter from Winnie in England beginning with the ominous, "Tim's parents asked me to write this letter." Tim had committed suicide. What had happened was that Tim had taken a long walk and fallen half in the creek and couldn't get up out of the mire.

A search party looked for him all night and only found him in the morning. He contracted severe pneumonia and was hospitalized. I visited him and he was proud to have made you pregnant. I helped him get a lawyer so he could provide for you and leave his armed services pension to the child. The pension is small but better than nothing. It helps that we have one from Harold's perilous service in World War I. He still has difficulties from the mustard gas. Anyway, Tim was getting better but then he got a severe case of flu from the hospital air. He shrank to nothing. He saved up his pills in secret, took them all at once, and committed suicide. It was too much to ask him to stay alive. He was suffering horribly. I'm sorry to have to tell you this. He gave me this little note for you.

Winnie had enclosed the note which read, "I'm so happy that you are pregnant. I am sorry I won't see the child. Maybe in the afterlife if there is one. I could no longer bear life as it is given me. I love you. Tim."

She sat in the barnyard on the milk stool and wept for an hour or so which also made Hud moan and wail. She finally stopped and took him for a walk out in the pasture where he touched noses with the calves. They both seemed to enjoy this. Then he reverted to his true character and killed a harmless garter snake and ate it with evident relish. She would have to redouble her efforts to train him away from snakes.

She hoped to have twins and get childbearing over with in one effort. Two was the perfect number of children. François came out from Florida in the early fall. He was mortally disappointed that there would be no lovemaking for the time being. He said that he had driven two thousand miles for nothing to which she answered, "You might have called first." She told him the whole story and broke down again at Tim's suicide. He was consoling. He had brought along two female English setters, both spayed, and Hud was frantically interested but they both bit him, their "keep away" signal, and he seemed puzzled and hurt to have his affection painfully rejected. François had fine hunting for Hungarian partridge, sharp-tailed grouse, and a few ruffed grouse. They ate very well though she couldn't drink any of the case of wine he brought aside from a sip or two because it made her queasy. He was a fine cook and she acted as sous-chef playing Mozart as always as she cooked. He stayed five days and she knew that she could make love but she had a terrifying fear of miscarriage. When he left he promised to visit every fall which made her happy.

She entered a long period of lassitude caused by the constant morning illness. She did nothing but read, and of late she reread the novels of Lawrence Durrell and Malcolm Lowry, two of her current favorites, and she continued with her many anthologies of Chinese poetry. She liked the Chinese notion that the most fortunate life was one in which nothing much happened. She liked to sit at the kitchen window and watch dawn arrive in the barnyard, pleased that the baby was making her fatter. She had been moderately slender and it was interesting to develop large breasts. She looked at them in the mirror and thought it would be nice to keep them around after the baby but such wasn't possible. Jerry had offered to send her to any graduate school she wished if she wanted to become a lawyer or doctor. When she said she only wanted to be a farmer, he couldn't quite believe this lack of ambition though all he himself had ever done was spend money. Ambition didn't really trouble Catherine. Since earliest childhood she just wanted to be on a farm, like her mother except that Catherine had succeeded. Jerry every year was written up in socialite magazines as

a high-net-worth individual but in Catherine's mind that
didn't seem to do her mother any good, at least not as much
as feeding the chickens did for Catherine. It was an antique
question at best but the significant thing in life was whether
or not your soul was at peace. Catherine felt hers was and
now it looked like she was going to get to raise the child
she so much wanted.

Chapter 12

In late fall Catherine's mother showed up on only a few days' notice, she said to "help with the baby" though it wasn't due for another couple of weeks. Catherine was appalled at the presumption but prepared the upstairs bedroom her mother favored. Catherine had a very early memory of loving sleeping upstairs with her mother, how the stones she would heat up in cold weather would warm the bed. They would get up at 5:00 a.m., do chores with Grandpa, and then eat a big breakfast in the warm kitchen beside the wood range her grandparents cooked on. Catherine liked it best when Grandpa would squirt milk directly from the cow's udder into the open mouths of the barn cats. She wanted to learn this trick as a little girl but her hands only became strong enough to milk a cow when she was older.

That first evening was enervating. She could see her mother's depression through her face tight from plastic surgery. Earlier she had watched the sun go down through the kitchen window.

"This was what I always wanted and didn't get." Her voice was muted and without its usual hardness.

"It's not too late. You're only in your fifties," Catherine replied.

Her mother gave her the look of one who had driven into a deep gully and never considered any alternatives for getting out. Like many women growing older she was an utter fatalist.

"I wrote many times to Robert in person apologizing and he finally answered saying he forgave me. But I'm unsure about forgiveness. Look what we did to him."

"I'm unsure of why I survived and Robert didn't. Dad picked on him and ignored me until Robert ran away. Then it was too late. When a child learns mistrust it's hard to overcome it." Catherine felt tears form in her eyes.

Her mother took a vodka shooter out of her purse and finished it in one swallow. "I still haven't quit though the doctors said I must," she said.

"Why do they want you to?"

"My liver is a mess among other things."

"You better quit. It's hard for a liver to recover." Her mother actually looked very good for her age.

"I keep myself slim but what else can I do? We have servants for everything. Jerry hates it when I do dishes."

"That's absurd."

"I know it. He grew up with a critical mother. He's so worried that I might complain about something. I told him I was coming out here to help with the baby and buy a farm to fulfill my girlhood ambition. He said, 'Go ahead.' You of course know that your father broke his promise to me that we would live on a farm. He wanted to wear a tie and work in a bank. He said that he was belittled in school for being a farm kid."

"I doubt that. What else is there around here but farm kids? A few army brats. Gas station owners. Grocery store owners and clerks."

"I learned never to believe anything he said. Your grandfather despised him, said he was a chiseler. His own son. How could it be that his own son could redefine ineptitude?"

"Well, he wasn't about a great hero, but . . ." Catherine was uncomfortable speaking ill of the dead.

"When you two kids were little I should have grabbed you and run for it. It was cowardly I didn't."

Later that evening when Catherine went up to bed she wondered if her mother might be ill and had come on this visit to Montana as a last chance to ask for forgiveness. Catherine didn't know what to think. She saw life as more of a constant whirl in which people often behaved horribly. What was the point of forgiving the early whirls? She knew she would forgive her if her mother asked, however, thinking there was nothing else to do. The past lives on in all of us. No matter how wronged we were the offenses were only the beaten-up junk of memory, pawed over until they were without color if still somehow alive. Late that evening her mother began weeping, she said over Robert in prison, but Catherine doubted it, thinking that it must be the entirety of life.

"We had such fun when I brought you out here as a little girl. At the time you treated the chickens as if they were the biggest mystery in life."

"Maybe they are, along with humans. I liked going out to the dark barn with Grandpa at five a.m. Then when it got fully light I'd feed the chickens. I guess at heart we all like to be useful. Even now Hudley likes his breakfast early. If I don't feed him by seven he starts barking like crazy."

After her cereal next morning Mother took Hud for a walk to his beloved bone pile out behind the barn. Hud already adored her and they settled into a routine where she'd take him for his early morning walk. In the evenings he slept at the end of Alicia's bed and warmed it up which meant she didn't have to carry the warm stones up the steep stairs, but Hud would bark if she didn't. It also meant that he no longer expected to sleep with Catherine which was a relief. He would trot up and down the stairs with her under the illusion that he was helping. She wouldn't allow Catherine to give her a hand, saying her legs needed the exercise.

One morning while they were out Catherine called Jerry. He was appalled that her mother hadn't told her yet that she had ovarian cancer and he hoped she would last long enough to help Catherine with the baby. After the baby was born they would meet at the Mayo Clinic in Rochester, Minnesota, to try and prolong her life. Jerry had hoped to help nurse her too but she said she was overrun with help. He hinted he would like to be invited out for a visit. Catherine said, "Come ahead," and he was there in a few days. He came by private jet and they picked him up at the Texan's

landing strip next door. She still disliked the neighbor but
money knew how to talk to money apparently.

Jerry was an immediate pain in the ass insisting that
he have a new house built for Catherine and the baby. Catherine simply enough didn't want it. She liked the old one but
settled on Jerry having a master bedroom wing built with
an adjoining room for the baby. The contractor was there
in the morning. By the looks of Catherine's belly time was
of the essence so Jerry offered the contractor extra money
for speed. The contractor broke into an easy smile seeing
Christmas come early.

Jerry was so overbearing in looking after her mother
that it drove both women batty. Luckily he became quite
bored with the farm and said at the second dinner that he
needed to fly to Key West. Catherine assumed it was to see
his girlfriend. Jerry had drunk most of a bottle of Scotch that
late afternoon and his slurred speech grated on her nerves.
They were both enormously relieved in the morning when
the Texan's hired hand picked him up for his plane with its
twelve seats and leather sofa. He was gaining a lot of weight
and Catherine watched from the window as he waddled to
the car. Catherine knew that he never read and wondered
what he and her mother talked about. Recent purchases?
She could see that age would eventually make him disgust-
ing but with ovarian cancer her mother wouldn't see it. She
had obviously had bad luck with men when you overlooked
Jerry's wealth. Money was nearly meaningless to Catherine
even though she knew she would enjoy a big bedroom and
a baby room attached to the house. The door would be off
the kitchen, her favorite room. She used to play cribbage

at the kitchen table with a maiden great-aunt who lived her last year with the grandparents. She worked in Chicago as a young woman and when they played cards the radio in the evening was tuned to a station there. She nattered constantly about the beauty of Chicago and made Catherine promise to go there when she grew up. Catherine was even now embarrassed that when she had visited Chicago she stayed in the Drake where her maiden aunt had worked.

Of late Catherine who was not of a religious bent wondered what became of Tim after suicide. Christians would say that suicides went directly to hell, wherever that was. It was left over from Sunday school she supposed. Catherine was unsure of hell or an afterlife but thought his lifelong pain should count for something. She had watched a local man limping on the sidewalk. He had lost his toes to the cold in Korea. It could have been worse and local lazy people envied his disability payments. Something for nothing was the ultimate good as far as they were concerned. War was hardly nothing. She regretted not being able to help Clyde load the hay bales onto the wagon and then into the barn because of her pregnancy.

Mother wept for a couple of days and then in a torrent of garbled language apologized to Catherine for the abuses in her raising. The first duty, she said, of a mother is to protect her children, even from her husband. Her own husband had never gotten out of himself for even a moment. Once assured of Catherine's forgiveness her mother declined dramatically as if this forgiveness had been her life's work. Catherine called Jerry in Key West saying that the situation was serious. Jerry said he'd try to get away. She thought, From

your fishing and adulterous fucking. Meanwhile, she had to
get her mother several appointments with a psychiatrist in
the county seat because she was plainly becoming daft. She
would sit on the front porch talking to Robert who was obviously not there. She drove her mother the two hours to the
prison to visit Robert but her mother couldn't complete the
mission. She vomited in the parking lot seeing the walls and
razor wire fencing. She was catatonically angry. "Why put
him here just because he burned that piece of shit house?"
Catherine had tried to explain Robert's refusal to fight for
himself. By the time of the fire her ex-husband's illusions had
plainly gotten out of hand. He was pretending he was "old
money" living in a grand home though he was borrowing
gin money from hunting acquaintances. Catherine figured
that his delusions came from a lifetime of hard drinking.

Chapter 13

Catherine drove Jerry and her mother to the Texan's landing strip. The Texan had only dropped Jerry off the day before in his new Jeep Wagoneer. No one local would use a six-thousand-dollar vehicle to roam his ranch. Catherine was glad to see them leave, flying east to Rochester, Minnesota, to get her mother admitted to Mayo. Her mother sobbed piteously while boarding the plane because she couldn't stay to help with the oncoming baby. Help by being a relentless pain in the ass? Catherine thought wryly. You couldn't miss Jerry's self-importance in boarding a private jet.

She daily felt heavier and more awkward but was pleased when the baby kicked in her womb. She could barely make her morning stroll with Hud out to the pond and boneyard behind the barn. One day it was cool and rainy and she refused to go and he actually wept until she relented, bundled in a sweater and raincoat. She reminded herself of the perils of starting habits with dogs. In the big pasture they had to go back every time to the rock pile where he had once almost but not quite caught a big black snake. He was obviously goaded by his failure.

Near the pond she sat on a big rock with a peculiar resemblance to a monster stone egg. It had been Catherine's "magic" place since early childhood. When she frequently visited the farm with her mother she'd walk out to her stone egg when she was disturbed by anything and the stillness of the scene pacified her. How can you draw pure energy from a stone? It was possible for her. Later in life it occurred to her that in the serenity of the place she had arrived at a point of child meditation where her mind emptied itself of its enervating trash and she could identify with the pond and big pile of white cow bones. Now it amused her when Hud tried to pick up the pelvis of a cow skeleton. His jaws weren't strong enough yet to pick it up but he had slowly dragged it about halfway to his trophy hideout in the front yard lilac grove. Such extreme effort for his own private reasons. Like a child he had his own collection of "stuff" whose importance was clear only to the owner.

She sat there on the stone egg and was flooded with rare sympathy for her mother. Her father's promise of a farm in Montana was an outrageous lie and it was obvious that he'd never had any intention of keeping that promise. Her grandfather in England told her that her father was a "scoundrel." Who in his right mind would rather run a tiny bank than be a farmer? This was during a long conversation during the Blitz. Her grandparents had urged their daughter early on to leave the bastard but along came Robert and her.

Even his own parents were not that fond of him, preferring the company of Catherine's mother. She was always absolutely welcome at the farm but it would have been a small town scandal had she moved out there permanently. Now Catherine believed that she should have. What did it really matter if her mother had embraced her singular desire? It was a brutal lesson indeed to both mother and daughter. To live at a distance of a half dozen miles from where your heart was.

As she sat there scratching Hud's ears which he loved the worry about Tim was nagging at her, this idea that suicides must go to hell. It was maddening to worry about a person already dead and she couldn't quite believe that God would add to the suffering of someone who had already suffered so much. To her the suicide had been an act of courage. To deny the self further existence when the self had been so rended. War waits to kill some.

She wanted to examine her religious beliefs and discard the ones that no longer made sense but it seemed difficult when she was this pregnant. She also perceived that to discard them wouldn't be all that easy or simple. They were ingrained. When she was passionately religious as a young girl she read the Gospels over and over. By contrast the Old Testament was mean and foreboding. Why did King David so desire Bathsheba and send her husband away to be killed in battle? That seemed very mean-minded to her and Laura had agreed. And why did this great man peek at Bathsheba while she was bathing? This was definitely a sin she supposed. Even now she said her prayers before bed in the evening though they were quite abbreviated. She kept recalling her disappointment as a girl when she prayed that her parents would quit getting drunk and it hadn't happened. She still believed devoutly in the Resurrection partly because it was such a glorious, magical idea to rise from the dead with the spike scars in your hands and feet. She knew that a belief in magic was quite common among her friends, even her Sunday school teacher who claimed to have seen several ghosts.

Now to Catherine the magic of life was in the spectacular assortment of species. Even at this moment she saw the nose of a muskrat rise above the surface of the pond. Hud also saw it and sitting beside her quivered with excitement but then he was thinking of a wild meal. She had read that some people ate muskrats from the river in Detroit, Michigan, but then she had also read that poor people in the Southwest ate donkeys during the Depression. Why God had decided not to stop her parents' drinking was the early question that stuck with her. It seemed a simple request but then that was long before she knew anything about addiction. She herself had been truly drunk only once on her college graduation night and felt badly for three days which prevented her from doing it again. It had competed with the preposterous discomfort of being nearly nine months pregnant. She had read once about a woman who bore eighteen children which now seemed thoroughly incomprehensible even if she had been a cow.

Chapter 14

Catherine summoned Clyde one Sunday morning for a somewhat formal meeting on the farm after her walk. She needed him to spend more time around her place in case she fell and delivered the baby on the ground. The obstetrician had warned her to be more cautious about her walking for the time being.

In fact Catherine was finding walking difficult now. Her legs and feet hurt from the extra weight. She thought now that one baby would certainly be enough. She kept recalling how she had ruined walking for a while way back when she was doing the Lorca project in college. The poet had obviously spent a great deal of time walking around the city for *Poet in New York* and her plan was to imitate the tactic. One morning she started out on 112th Street and walked all the way to Washington Square in the Village where she felt lucky to hear a very good violinist play a Paganini piece that was a little beyond him but not by far. He smiled as spectators filled his open violin case with money. A dapper old man dropped in a twenty and the musician broke into a grin.

Now back at the farm Clyde seemed nervous like all of the poor about a good job. He finally blurted out that when Jerry was here he had stopped by and asked Clyde if he thought he could handle managing the Texan's ranch in addition to Catherine's farm. Clyde thought it over briefly and said yes because the Texan's ranch was a basic cow operation where you turned bulls loose every year and then waited to see how many new calves you got. Of course there were a thousand somewhat complicated details but none that Clyde couldn't handle.

Catherine felt up in the air about the whole business though she knew it would be good for Clyde making him a big shot manager of a large ranch. The poor are always saying, "I'd like a break that is not my neck." So she told Clyde she was pleased for him. She couldn't add that she could barely stand the sight of Jerry. But then she predicted to herself that he wouldn't be out that often. His sport was buying, not maintaining what he bought. He might go to one Cattlemen's meeting to strut a bit and that would largely be it. She told Clyde to make sure he kept a good set of books because the rich thrive on the suspicion that they are being swindled.

Chapter 15

When she went into labor Clyde drove her to the new little hospital in Livingston (her mother had insisted she go to the big hospital in Bozeman but as usual she ignored her). The pains were still far apart and she noticed that it was December 7, the anniversary of Pearl Harbor. If it was a daughter maybe she should name it "Pearl" but then she never had cared for the name. Catherine had been so consumed by the Blitz she never thought about Pearl Harbor except once she had seen a photo of a big ship the Japanese had sunk and couldn't imagine it on the ocean floor.

It was a long delirious day until early in the evening when she gave birth, a difficult breech birth, to a boy. She held the homely little runt for a few minutes and thought of the William Blake line, "Little lamb, who made thee." She was still possessed with some of the horrifying aspects of giving birth, hallucinating herself as a huge, opening tropical flower with a fatally injured core. She wondered if that meant she was dying and she would see Tim in the after-life but was quite relieved when it didn't happen and they brought her the cottage cheese she had requested. Birth was hard work and she was hungry. She recalled when she finally reached Greenwich Village one day on a particularly long hike for Lorca she went to a little Italian place she knew and had pasta with marinara and one big meatball. She relished it. Typical of her obstinacy she turned around and walked all the way back, the last hour in a steady chilly rain so she returned to the apartment with aching legs in the guise of a wet dog. Her roommate was appalled and put her to bed after a bowl of chicken soup. She woke the next morning with shin splints, unable to walk to class. There's something in cement that doesn't love a foot, she thought, but New Yorkers must get used to it. You certainly don't get shin splints walking in a pasture.

She called her mother. Alicia wasn't doing well at all according to Jerry who answered the phone. She told him she had named the baby Tim. He congratulated her and her mother came on the line for a few minutes and in a weak voice said, "I wish I were there to help you."

Chapter 16

It was a tough winter with the baby who had colic. Only dancing would slow his crying. She questioned her indomitable will to reproduce deciding its origins were too far beneath the skin to comprehend. Clyde's wife Clara and her two daughters came over and stayed a couple of weeks to help out. The older daughter Laurel said she didn't like babies but she turned out to be the most helpful with little Tim. He had lost the red face of a newborn and now was pale with black hair like his father. Catherine had given the baby all that she was and then some. As she had with Tim. She felt unbearably depressed, the so-called "baby blues," so she took a lot of vitamins and made sure she at least walked out to the pond and back every morning. It seemed to improve slightly with the solstice and on sunny winter days, of which there are many in Montana, she clocked the ever so slight increase of light with the specific shadows of the barn. She remembered from her childhood that after the hard work of autumn, harvest and butchering, everyone became happier after the solstice and the long, sure trek toward spring. Her solstice reverie was interrupted by a big blizzard at Christmas and she was relieved she was well stocked with groceries and didn't have to drive anywhere. She felt especially sorry for those who felt compelled to make long driving trips for Christmas.

Nursing was a great pleasure. She was becoming too thin and devised ways to make up for it. She mentioned aloud that she so missed the sausages of her grandparents who were fine sausage makers, burying their product in a huge crock of pig fat to preserve it like the French do their confit. Clyde told her there was a new, cranky young butcher in Livingston. The roads were still bad but she had bought a big diesel pickup for the farm and he returned with five pounds of sausage and a big beef roast for Christmas dinner. It was a happy occasion and Catherine made Yorkshire pudding as her mother had done. Her mother had been a deeply mediocre and hasty cook, and her ability further declined the more she drank. Catherine had noticed that the good cooks she knew saved their drinks for after the dishes were prepared except men at the barbecue, a great deal easier than any of them were prone to admit. Following a few principles they managed even when half drunk.

Jerry called to say Mother had died Christmas Day at Mayo. This was three days later but he said he hadn't wanted to ruin her Christmas. They might have been able to prolong things a little longer but she had a horror of oxygen and feeding tubes and had asked them when it reached that point to "pull the plug." Jerry also said she had written a note asking that her ashes be strewn on the pond behind the barn, and that she wanted Catherine to do it.

Unlike with her father Catherine wept for a while. When she was a little girl she and her mother would have picnics on the pond, squinting their eyes and pretending it was a big lake. On the especially hot days of summer they would bathe in the pond which was sandy around the edges. Only when not around her husband could her mother be utterly pleasant. Catherine mourned what might have been. She was convinced now that her mother should have taken her and Robert back to England and raised them in London. Her parents had offered to take them in, she later told Catherine, which was what led to their visit before war broke out.

Her obstetrician had sent her an antique Lakota papoose for Christmas and she packed Tim warmly inside for morning walks. Her neighbor had cleared her driveway with his tractor and plow and she had him scrape out an area to throw feed to the chickens. She had a small stroller for Tim and shoveled a path from the house for the stroller. By March Tim's first laughter had been at the chickens. Hud, who was getting much larger, would sit beside the stroller as if he were a guard, typical of the breed, and growl deeply at approaching chickens who feared him.

In April on a warmish day the snow seemed to be melting. Catherine was out in the barnyard with Tim having a sandwich and feeding him a jar of pureed peaches, watching the nearly mature hatchlings driving each other batty. Tim watched them closely and didn't stop smiling. She held him up at the fence so he could touch the soft noses of the horses and a single very docile calf. Clyde had come by with three piglets to raise good pork for the two households. She had long figured out that supermarket pork wasn't nearly as tasty as what her grandfather had home raised and butchered. It would cost money to feed them as you couldn't grow corn easily in this high, dry climate. Hud growled and the piglets shrank back in the pen. Tim reached out for them but Catherine held him back thinking they might mistake his little hand for food. Three days later one of the piglets got out but only trotted over to nibble corn scratch with the chickens. Tim was gleeful and Hud furious. She said, "Hud, no," to his growling. She was able to pet the piglet and scratch its ears, both of which it liked. Tim was so delighted to touch its ears and the piglet sniffed his hand.

In grade school the boys who all dressed like junior cowboys had called her a "wimp" for her tenderhearted view of the lowliest creatures. Her mother had given her Charles Roberts's *The Naturalist's Diary* for her birthday. Her concern was widespread and it seemed that every boy craved to shoot a deer, elk, moose, bear, anything would do in the local ethic. Only one mannerly boy was interested in bird dogs and hunting for Hungarian partridge and sharp-tailed grouse with his father. She had a crush on him but he ignored girls. Catherine's mother was also softhearted about animals. She convinced her to let go a turtle she had caught in the cattails at the edge of the pond. Her mother's point was "Why should the turtle's only life be to amuse you?" Her mother had studied biology in England but was largely unaware of American wildlife. On an early trip south to

Yellowstone her parents had seen a sow grizzly kill an elk. Her father thought they were lucky to see it but her mother was totally repelled and had grizzly nightmares. The junior cowboys loved to scare each other and the girls with stories about rattlesnakes and grizzlies. A boy in her sixth-grade class was bitten in the arm by a baby rattler in the school woodlot. His arm had become horribly swollen but they got him to the hospital in time for the antivenom to be effective. She was shocked and told her father about it at dinner. He laughed saying that boys get bitten because they're always fooling with snakes to show their daring, same as when he was young. This was why she was trying to aversion train Hud to rattlers. She had used a choke collar for a few weeks whenever they saw snakes and now on the rare occasion when they saw one on a walk he would shrink back and whine. There were no grizzlies in the Crazy Mountains nearby but there were some in the Absaroka Mountains less than fifty miles to the south. There was a written record of Lewis and Clark killing one locally when they passed through. Catherine had hiked with friends in the Absarokas but had never seen a grizzly and hadn't wanted to see one.

Jerry called to say that he was sending her mother's ashes by Purolator courier adding that she should go ahead and distribute the ashes by the "lake" as he had an important business trip to make for several weeks in Key West. It took her breath away. The heel. He couldn't be bothered. She felt a flash of anger that upset her stomach.

The next day the ashes arrived and along with them a check for fifty thousand dollars with "Tim's education" written in the memo field. She guessed Jerry was buying off his conscience. She didn't care. Did he have to fly to Key West to get laid? Surely someone closer to New York would make sense, or the summer place in Rhode Island where the entryway was cold marble. She would put the money in the bank where it would reproduce and Tim could go off in eighteen years in new clothes. What more could she want of life? She had no lover but certainly didn't want one for the time being. But she had a farm, a few horses, about fifty cattle, three piglets, and of course the beloved chickens, also a tiny boy who seemed to like them too. The other day she stupidly ran to the house for the phone and left Hud to guard Tim. When she returned a hatchling was nestled in his diaper and he was smiling from ear to ear while Hud growled at it. Catherine had taught Hud to stay clear of the hatchlings though it enraged him when they pecked at his feet. With one hand Tim brushed the feathers with little coos.

Another piglet escaped, and she called Clara who caught it with difficulty, finally offering it more scratch which it ate out of her hand.

"Doesn't make you want to eat pork, does it?"

"No!" Catherine laughed. It was best not to name a pig or cow who would end up as meat. The piglet squealed in anger when Clara put him back in the pen and plugged up the escape hole. He simply wanted to wander around freely.

Chapter 17

The parents of a ten-year-old Mexican girl had died locally in a car accident and the township was looking for a foster parent who spoke Spanish to take care of her until relatives came from Mexico to retrieve her at the end of the summer, some months away. It was commonly known that Catherine was the only white person in the area who spoke Spanish and she had a decision to make. A recent cold snap had left snow on the ground and Catherine shivered on her way to meet the girl, Lola, and a social worker at the drugstore for a chocolate sundae. The girl held Tim and then quickly changed his diaper on the counter. Her deftness won Catherine's heart. She spoke soft sibilant Spanish to Tim who enjoyed it. At dinnertime the social worker brought Lola out to the farm. Hud had taken off across the pasture that afternoon and not come back but she couldn't look for him with the girl arriving. She was sure he'd be all right. Lola had a pathetically small amount of belongings. Her English was fair and full of American slang. She was amused by Catherine's Spanish and called her "profesora." Catherine put her into her old bedroom adjoining the new addition so she could hear Tim.

The next morning it felt as warm as a Chinook wind as she looked out at the distant Crazy Mountains, named for the woman who had gone fatally crazy there. Catherine remembered the Chinooks of her childhood fondly. Once it was only ten degrees in the early morning and by noon it was sixty. Kids at school loved them and ran around in shirtsleeves.

Lola looked after Tim, playing with him on the living room rug where he shrieked with laughter, while Catherine carried her mother's ashes out behind the barn across the lingering snow. She sat on her egg rock holding the box of ashes inside of which was a lovely urn, no doubt Jerry's idea. There was a thin lid of ice on the pond which was quickly melting. She cast the first handful of ashes out on the ice feeling with her fingers and seeing small bits of bone which was eerie. She was able to take off her coat in the warm wind. She continued to toss handfuls of ashes saying, "Goodbye, Mother." How could her mother become ashes? She reminded herself of the ways of the earth.

When she finished and the ashes were sinking into the water she thought about how much her mother loved this place and all of their early little picnics. Now the two horses and a calf and a cow were watching her over the fence with curiosity. She would try to keep Tim off of horses for as long as possible. The area was full of the maimed and injured from horseback accidents. Other places boys wanted to be football and basketball stars but here they wanted to be heroes of rodeo, much more dangerous even than football.

Suddenly, with both her parents gone she felt like an orphan and missed her grandparents in London. When she had called her grandmother about her mother's death Catherine kept sobbing and whispering, "It's not fair." Of course it wasn't. It had been more than a decade since she had turned to her parents for anything. So many people she knew carried their parents around in emotional backpacks. Her own story was largely unknown to anyone but herself and Robert in prison whose sentence had recently been lengthened for beating up a guard. This was plainly the curse of the father. She herself felt no curse and had often thought that her early trip to England to see her grandparents had successfully detoxified her life. She would fly over this summer so they could see their great-grandson and she would also visit Tim's family. They were getting very old and had just lost their only child. She planned to take Lola with her to help with the baby.

Thoughts of Robert reminded Catherine of another childhood experience that had started as a truly horrid summer evening. Her father had been drunk and raged about stock market losses which he blamed on the "Jews." Catherine and her mother didn't believe anything he said and ignored him so he fixed his anger on Robert. They had been eating at the picnic table in the backyard and her father had fallen down twice trying to chase Robert. Robert was much faster which further enraged him. He demanded Robert stop so he could beat him but Robert cut through the hedge and was headed downtown. After dark he came home and thought it was safe because peeking through the window he saw his father was asleep on the den couch. Robert came up to Catherine's room and said that he was running away at dawn. She said she wanted to go along. She got up and made several peanut butter and jelly sandwiches to take. Robert filled his Boy Scout canteen, packed a day pack with warm clothes, and rolled up his summer sleeping bag. After midnight Father awoke, went to Robert's room, and beat him. Catherine's mother tried to stop him and he pushed her to the floor. Robert's lip was cut from a punch and there was blood. Catherine went into the room and screamed, "Daddy, stop that!" The scream was so penetrating that he stopped and walked out the door. That cinched their departure.

They left in the first scant light of dawn walking north to a big woods to conceal themselves if they were being followed. By midday they were lost despite Robert's Scout compass. They were headed toward Martinsdale where Robert had a friend. Their feet hurt and they spread the sleeping bag and slept a couple of hours in the heat of the afternoon. They hogged their sandwiches but were still hungry. Robert judged that they were too high in the foothills of the Crazy Mountains. They continued to walk, refilling their canteen in a safe-looking creek. They both knew the danger of giardia from animal waste in the water. Late in the afternoon she was sure she recognized parts of the landscape. She mentioned this to Robert who became angry realizing that like many lost people they had walked in a big circle and they were now about two miles behind Grandpa's farm. They had circled all the way back to the southeast.

When they reached the pond Robert built a small fire
and they heated a can of baked beans, all that was left of
their food supplies. She ordinarily didn't like them but on
this evening they were delicious. They snuggled up in the
sleeping bag near the fire where Grandpa found them at
dawn.

Catherine remembered this fondly twenty-five years
after the fact. Mother drove out to pick them up. She had
a black eye. Dad had pounded on her until she called the
deputy who hauled Dad off to the jail in Livingston where
he would be spending a second night. He never forgave her
for the public shame of this.

Catherine tilted the urn to the side and dumped out the
rest of the ashes into the water. Her finger touched what was
obviously a piece of vertebra and she felt a chill. She felt
oddly serene sitting there until she thought that she must go
back to the house and feed Tim his lunch. Hud was asleep,
tired from his night of wandering. She would have Clyde
build a pen to contain him at night when he wasn't sleeping
inside because of bad weather. He was having a pretty good
life with her and little Tim and now Lola who was obsessed
with sweeping the floors. Hud already fawned over Lola and
Catherine remembered the man's joke about interspecies
love as she passed the chicken yard. There she had sat in
the second grade, making notes outside the henhouse while
sitting on the milk stool.

The Case of the
Howling Buddhas

From his upstairs bedroom at 6:00 a.m. Sunderson could dimly hear his cell phone in his jacket pocket down in his study. It was more irritating then getting up to pee on a cold night. He was proud of the way his prostate was holding up at his age, also of his ears and their acute hearing in an era when many had destroyed their hearing with loud rock music.

The phone calls had been nearly continuous since 5:00 a.m. and he wanted to jerk the caller's teeth out with his Griplock pliers. He normally arose shortly before 7:00 a.m., flipped the coffee machine on, and went to his study, pulled out a book from the shelf that blocked the window, and gazed at his neighbor Delphine doing her nude yoga. She knew he was watching and was enthused because it helped what she called "sexual repression." Last Thursday she had masturbated in plain view, then called to say that her husband had gone to East Lansing and they could enjoy themselves. He hustled over to the back door in his old terry-cloth robe and she met him in her bare skin smelling of Camay soap.

Sunderson was ready early with his coffee and had pulled a study titled *The Jongleurs* for his view. She was flat on her tummy in a position called Snake's Pose, one of his favorites as it showed her sumptuous ass and the concealed goodies. In the year or so they had been playing the game her husband had showed up only once to make love to her. Sunderson had quickly replaced the book. He didn't want to start the day seeing a nude man, always a laughable sight. Her husband was a stiff who taught American literature at the local university. She taught anthropology and was tremendously popular with students while these same students ignored a course of her husband's devising called "Faulkner vs. Hemingway," as if the two writers had been in a footrace. He had told Sunderson that he had hoped to become the department chairman and perhaps a dean someday. He was without apparent personality and she had told Sunderson that he had some money on the side which afforded them the opportunity to spend their summers in Europe. That was why she married him. The money enabled her to visit archaeological digs in southern France and Spain. Her academic career was limited because she had never finished her Ph.D. dissertation despite working on it for fourteen years. Her excuse was that her mentor professor at Cornell had died and no one else was capable of dealing with her complicated writing.

Sunderson had noted that his voyeurism lacked the punch it had when he was watching his young ex-neighbor Mona, whom his ex-wife had later adopted, in her nude calisthenics. His neighbor shifted into the Royal Flux with her legs flopped up and over her head. He actually yawned rather than feeling his worm turn. He was not prone to fully accepting aging though he knew very well that it was what caused his sexuality to be less than rampant.

The other day on a warm afternoon he was sitting on the front porch reading the paper, the *Mining Gazette*, when Barbara, a lovely girl from down the street, broke her bicycle chain in front of his house. He fetched his pliers and small hammer from the kitchen and fixed it, removing a link. It was too loose anyway. Meanwhile she squatted in front of him with her weight on her haunches. It was simply electrifying with her bare lovely legs under the blue skirt leading upward to the white undies with a slight indication of pubic hair. He was naturally engrossed and tarried at the simple job. She had done well in the state high school gymnastics championships but was lithe rather than short and muscular like most female gymnasts.

"There you are," he said, finishing the job.

"Did you enjoy the view?" she asked coquettishly.

"Yes, frankly, it was wonderful," he said taking a last look before she got up.

"My uncle Bob will sit on a chair for an hour if I'm on the sofa with my dress up a little. It's really quite funny."

"It's the nature of man," Sunderson said self-righteously. She had to be sixteen and above the age of consent.

"Boys are terrible now. All they want day after day is blow jobs." She was apparently eager to talk about sex.

"Well, I suppose you avoid pregnancy."

"I simply don't like it one bit. I'm saving for college if you have any work you need done. I'm good at weeding. I get two bucks an hour."

"I have a flower garden that needs work when you have time."

"Sure thing." She hiked up her dress to throw a leg over the bike seat, a view which gave him a jolt. She smiled and rode off.

She hadn't returned as of yet. He meant to have her rake some leaves which he loathed doing. People in Munising used to be cheapskates. You'd rake for hours and get blisters on your hands for a couple of quarters that you very much needed. He was always saving for another fishing reel he'd seen in the Montgomery Ward catalog.

It was a warm day for September and later that morning he saw Barbara in a pair of tan shorts in the grocery store buying a box of Cheerios. He imagined her eating from her bowl in her early morning nightie. When she saw him she cocked her hips and apologized for not yet taking care of his flowers saying, "Maybe this afternoon." He had no plans other than to watch the University of Michigan–Michigan State football game on television. When he got home he arranged a peeking laboratory up in his bedroom where a window looked out on the backyard flower garden. He adjusted its shade for concealment and polished his binoculars. Barbara made him lonesome for his ex-girlfriend Monica who had worked at the Landmark Inn in town, but now had

a boyfriend close to her own age, a college student at that.
Monica liked sex even more than he did and during their
months together he was frankly so worn out that he missed
a lot of the last week of trout season. Since Monica left a
couple of months before, he had made love twice to his ex-
wife Diane. He had had dinner at her place and been lucky
enough to see Mona, who was home for the weekend from
college, step out of the shower. He winced and ran for the
kitchen where he had a nasty glass of Diane's cooking sherry.

An insane desire occurred to him to go down on Barbara, as unlikely an idea as world peace. Did this call for
the services of a mind doctor? Sexual fantasies could easily
become tiresome, the mind migrated anywhere it could get
its nose tweaked. He defended himself with the contention
that Barbara was aesthetically overwhelming but even he
had to admit that this was truly lame. Her father was on
the city council and they had been at odds several times. He
was a classic liberal who was sure the police were forever
on the verge of taking away human rights from everyone.

He finally checked his cell for an explanation for all
of the irritating predawn calls. They were from Ziegler,
Marquette's only possible tycoon. When Sunderson was
still on the force and Ziegler's son was thirteen, one of his
friends had sneaked a five-pound joke turd, a true monster,
into their toilet at a party and Ziegler had called the station
demanding a police investigation to catch the guilty perp.
The captain had Sunderson answer the call because Sunderson was thought to have married well and therefore to
be a gentleman by the movers and shakers of the city. The
captain of course knew this was an illusion. Ziegler was a

local boy who had done phenomenally well, becoming an all-American tight end at the University of Michigan. He had graduated with high honors and his senior thesis had been published as a book. It was an exposé of his own family's turpitude in the mining business. When they came in contact, which was not often, Ziegler always pretended he couldn't remember Sunderson's name, an old tactic.

His son and twin girls were students at the University of Michigan. Mona had said they were typically perky rich kids. On the phone Ziegler said that one daughter was a problem and arranged to meet Sunderson on a street corner three blocks away. He was careful about appearances and didn't want people to see him consorting with a private detective. Sunderson met Ziegler's Lexus at the corner. He was obviously transfixed by two girls doing wheelies on their bikes at the intersection. One was a sprightly, handsome girl, the niece of the president of the university, and the other was Barbara, her light short skirt flipping up to her waist. Legs to die for, he thought. He knocked on Ziegler's window and got an irritated look then was beckoned into the car.

"I'd give thousands for a night with that one."

"Which one?" Sunderson teased.

"Don't fuck with me. I want those legs around my neck."

"I think she's underage. She lives three houses down the street from me."

"I don't give a shit. I'd take the chance. That's what lawyers are for."

"Her father is on the city council." Sunderson said this with an air of threat.

"I don't care. I can buy those little chickenshits for lunch."

Barbara rode close to the passenger seat, looked in the open window. "I'll be over in a little while after I pick up lemons for lemonade, darling."

"Why the fuck is she calling you darling? Why is she coming over?" Ziegler exploded.

"We're friends. She takes care of my flower garden."

"A big tough detective with a beautiful pussy weeding his flowers. That doesn't add up."

"A medium-size ex–state police detective with ten black belts in karate." He added the latter as manly decoration. Ziegler was restless as they danced around the main business.

"Here's the killer. I sent one of my daughters, Margaret, a check for three thousand to buy duds because she got all A's at the university. She signed over the check which was cashed by an organization called the Circle of Heaven and Hell. I had an old friend in the athletic department check it out. It's a Zen Buddhist group headed by a California kook. Now I'm not so dense that I don't know that Zen Buddhism is a time-honored group. But this cucaracha floated in with a costume of black robes and picked up a bunch of strays. He has them howling like monkeys."

"Monkeys?" Sunderson played dumb. Ziegler's wife had engaged Sunderson to look into the group when all three of the kids were involved, and he wanted to avoid reminding the man that he hadn't taken it all that seriously. He wondered why the athletic department.

"Yes. That was the report I got. I want you to look into this. Obviously I pay well."

That took care of that. It should be easy. He'd begin with Mona. She had looked into it before and he was sure she'd be up for it again. Meanwhile Ziegler implied he'd like to come over in order to see Barbara again. Sunderson, wanting privacy for his voyeurism, said that he had too much work to do.

"What does she wear?" Ziegler asked plaintively.

"Soft khaki short shorts. She's working on a tan."

Ziegler looked up at the sky through the windshield as if some answer might be there. He shook Sunderson's hand.

"Let me hear from you ASAP."

"Of course."

Sunderson walked hurriedly home to assume his upstairs perch. He reached the front porch just as Barbara pulled into the yard with a sack of lemons. He waved her into the house and followed her down to the hall into the kitchen with a sharp eye on her wagging butt cheeks.

"I'll work an hour or so then make lemonade. It's all that I'm eating. I'm trying to drop a few pounds." She patted her perfect butt as if it were overweight.

"Don't lose an ounce. Your butt is perfect."

"How do you know? You've never seen it. Maybe it's covered with acne," she said with a teasing grin.

"I'd appreciate a glance," he mumbled.

"I have to deal with my conscience. You don't. A divorced man is asking to see my ass. It seems harmless."

"It's an aesthetic exercise," he interjected.

"Oh well, Mr. Sunderson needs help." She turned and bent slightly, pulled down her shorts speedily, no undies, and then back up. "First you see it, then you don't," she laughed.

He had concentrated on taking an imaginary photo with his eyes. The butt was superb and he felt breathless with his heart pounding. "Once more, please."

"Not a chance. Maybe after my lemonade when I take my shower. I'm going sailing this afternoon." She was holding a pair of knee pads for weeding. "Let's make a deal. You get another look at the butt if you squeeze the lemons, and if you can help me with something I'm doing for a friend."

"Fair enough," he said as she hurriedly left the kitchen and went out the back door. Through the screen it was fetching when she bent over to put on her knee pads. A cautionary note flickered in his brain but failed to shine brightly. Toward the end of his relationship with Monica he had a drink with the prosecutor to discuss a case of vandalism at the local marina, where he'd done several big investigations in his time, and toward the end of the meeting the prosecutor had used the old expression "a word to the wise" which meant a bomb of some sort would drop. The upshot was the prosecutor claimed that he had received several complaints about Sunderson living with an underage girl. Her parents were both dead and that was why the case raised suspicion with local busybodies. Monica was actually nineteen, so there was no crime, but the prosecutor seemed to keep an eye on him after that.

Now here he was looking out his bedroom window at Barbara through binoculars. She was on her knees in the dahlias with her butt arched up like a beautiful house cat. He recalled that stupid song "Yummy Yummy Yummy (I got love in my tummy)." He felt suitably absurd. He recently had a lovely dinner with the new librarian for the solid pleasure of talking about books as he used to do with Diane. Now like a feeb he was waiting for another possible bare-butt viewing of Barbara when she had her lemonade. He felt a trace of shame. Act your age, he thought, but simply enough he didn't want to. He was an old boy on the loose again.

He called Mona in Ann Arbor, didn't get her, and left a long message until her voice mail lost its patience and cut out. Could they really howl like monkeys? He supposed he'd find out soon enough. Mona would enjoy snooping into this case.

The librarian hadn't excited him except for her mind. Of course she would be a far wiser seduction then Barbara. If he had been warned about Monica they were ready for his next misstep. He suspected a junior member of the police force of possibly stirring up trouble. He was known as the "Kid" because he looked very young and had been hired as liaison to the area's young people, something which he had trained for in college. The Kid had told Sunderson that his own thirteen-year-old sister had been sexually abused. Sunderson was curious because the Kid was obsessed with sexual abuse where there didn't seem to be any suggestion of it, much less evidence. He called a friend on the force in Saginaw from which the Kid hailed and found out there was in fact no sister. There was an early complaint against the Kid in high school from the mother of a neighbor girl who claimed that the Kid had tampered with her daughter. Sunderson's friend remembered this though no charges had been filed. He said that the Kid weepingly denied everything and although he was cleared he entered a long depression afterward. The Kid's father was a sergeant on the local force and not above beating the shit out of his son. Sunderson had no conclusions, only suspicions, but found ironic the Kid's zeal on sex cases and he had to be reprimanded for bringing so many cases with a very low conviction record.

Right now Sunderson was in a race against time. His fishing gear was packed near the front door and Marion was due in less than a half hour to go steelhead fishing on the Saint Marys River over in Sault Sainte Marie. Meanwhile, he had quickly squeezed the lemons and was aching to hear the downstairs shower shut off which would mean he was closer to another view. The thing she'd needed his help with was a hundred-dollar contribution to her friend's abortion fund. They were poor folks but her friends were raising the money so the mother could take her daughter down to Mount Pleasant in central Michigan for the procedure. Suddenly the shower went off and she was at the counter mixing her lemonade. He boldly reached out and palmed a buttock. His cell phone rang obnoxiously. He turned it off noting it was Mona in Ann Arbor whom he could call back. Barbara drank deeply and went into the living room, sitting down in a big red T-shirt she'd borrowed which came all the way down to mid-thigh. He knelt before her confidently pushing the shirt up to her waist. This was the world peace he was thinking about and he was right there when it was happening. He put his hands behind her knees and pushed them toward her chest. He put a big wet kiss on her vagina boring in with his tongue until she made a small squeak and said, "Oh my goodness" over and over. And then they heard the steps on the front porch and Marion called out for Sunderson. Marion later admitted that the sight of the girl's bicycle in the yard slowed him down a bit. Sunderson jumped up and nearly lost his balance falling backward. She deftly turned on the clicker tuning in one of many Saturday college football games. She pulled down the shirt and tried vainly to tidy herself.

"Hello, Barbara!" Marion practically exploded. Then he turned to Sunderson. "Barbara helped out in my office as a sixth grader. Now here she is almost all grown up."

Sunderson noted that Marion put an emphasis on "almost" then glared at him.

Barbara seemed nearly frozen in place. She smiled at Marion. "I took a shower after working in the garden. Now I'm getting dressed so I can go sailing with my friends."

Marion was polite enough to go into the kitchen and Sunderson followed after noting a wet spot on the back of Barbara's T-shirt. She rushed off while they stood in the kitchen drinking some of her lemonade.

"Let's go. We're burning up the day. I packed some pot roast sandwiches for a late lunch." While they loaded Sunderson's fishing gear Barbara said goodbye, throwing a lovely leg over the bicycle seat. Sunderson winced at his coitus interruptus.

In the car headed east toward the Soo Marion seemed a bit cool and critical. He had graduated from college in psychology and of course had been a teacher and principal for decades. Sunderson expected a lecture. They were barely out of Marquette on Route 28 when it began.

"Monica was one thing. Everyone found it scandalous but she was nineteen so you slid under the wire. Barbara is a totally different matter. She's *fifteen*. You're my oldest friend and I want you to exercise care so you don't end up in jail. There's no fishing in jail. She's a good kid and has no business wearing nothing but your T-shirt on the sofa. I can only guess what you were up to." Sunderson hurriedly told the story of his contribution to the abortion fund which made Barbara innocently affectionate to him.

"Oh bullshit," Marion exploded. "All the years I've known you you've had an eye out for young stuff. If I find out there's anything going on my next call is Barbara's parents and you're headed for the slammer. May I remind you they relate your syndrome to the unlived life? I know that in high school you were a wrestler and a bone-crunching linebacker. All the pretty girls like quarterbacks, running backs, and nice clean basketball players. You were left out by the pretty ones and even late in life you're hot on their track. Stop it. Period. Pursue Diane for Christ's sake. Or the neighbor lady. I don't care. Just don't let your dick lead you to jail or more likely prison."

They checked into the Ojibway so Sunderson could watch the ships pass through the huge Soo Locks, a long-time obsession. On the river there was a hard cold rain. Sunderson fished for an hour until he was shivering and soaking wet. He caught one six-pounder, enough for a good chowder. Marion had better rain equipment so he took Sunderson back to the hotel where they ate their delicious pot roast sandwiches with pickles and beer. Then Marion left to go back fishing. Sunderson ordered a pint of whiskey from room service to avoid walking back out in the rain to a liquor store. He remembered with fondness the lovely room service at the Arizona Inn in Tucson, also the breakfast at the Carlyle where he had set the stage to blackmail the rich mother of a rock musician who was dating Mona.

Thinking of Mona's rock 'n' roller who was now in a French prison after being caught with two underage girls made him nervous indeed. The most loathsome criminal of all was the pedophile. Sunderson considered fifteen years the cutoff, an adult woman in most of the world but America, except Louisiana. He could always go to New Orleans on the remaining supply of blackmail money but wasn't that admitting he was a sick cookie? He called Barbara out of impulse. She was on her bike but said she could talk. He said he was sorry they had been interrupted and she said, "Me too, I was really getting off. Of all people it was Principal Jones! I still owe you one." Sunderson, who was in bed to get warm, got an instant hard-on which proved to him that he might be hopeless. He was desperately afraid of prison. As a detective he had made a number of visits to Jackson Prison with its five thousand inmates, and to the local high-security prison in Marquette where the prisoners complained bitterly about the cold darkness of winter. He couldn't imagine anyplace more dismal. Out barred windows you could see stormy Lake Superior, often iced over in winter, not an attractive escape route. The solution was to fish and travel the rest of his life and avoid all young women. Stop now. Period. Maybe allow himself one more session with Barbara. But self-indulgence was always the problem—an ex-detective thinks he can get away with anything and soon he hasn't stopped at all. He needed to get a bird dog and return to hunting grouse and woodcock. But suddenly he was pondering the view with his photo image of

Barbara's delectable crotch as he went down on her on the sofa for a few minutes. The thought was needlessly electric and he despised his sense of being out of control. It was still months away from New Year's when an effective resolution might be made.

There had to be an escape route from this obsession. He loathed his mind's startling capacity to raise up an image of Barbara naked below the waist. Marion's lecture had given him a knot in his throat and his eyes were misting with frustration. He remembered the name of a mind doctor that Diane had given him. It might be time to bite the bullet and go, but would the man hold his information in confidence? It was hot info if it could send him to prison. What was it about our sexual impulses that demolished us and how did he end up with his ass in this sling? He had seen Barbara dozens of times on the block so why was he suddenly a witless ninny? Dante and Beatrice? Petrarch and Laura? A voice in him said, "Don't flatter yourself." A lovely girl is perched daintily on her haunches while he splices her bicycle chain and he is struck dumb, poleaxed, while looking up her legs. It was like peeing on an electric cattle fence which invariably knocked you to the ground, something city dwellers were pranked into doing while visiting their country cousins. Fistfights often followed.

He finally reached Mona. She was writing a paper about Machado, a Spanish poet she adored. Her look into Ziegler's situation revealed a striking mess. Mona had gone back into the group and reported that while one twin had lost interest and left the group the beloved pet daughter Ziegler had mentioned lived with the teacher-master and did the

cooking, an important position in the community. The three
grand her father sent doubtless went for food as the master
was quite a trencherman. Sunderson had also checked things
out with his ex-wife Diane who he remembered had been a
Zen student in college, purportedly a serious and traditional
student compared with the goofies in Ann Arbor at whom
Diane took serious umbrage. Sunderson knew from Diane
about Mona's many mental issues arising from college, her
distant father and worthless mother, and her rock 'n' roll
ex-lover. With Diane's encouragement Mona had become
interested in Zen as a way to try to resolve some of this.
Mona didn't mind deferring to authority which was part of
Zen, really more a total attitude than a religion. However,
Diane was rather strict on observances of over a thousand
years of tradition, stricter than her own Zen training in
college from what Mona told him. There was an American
tendency to try and adapt everything to our lack of customs.
If Mona said she was going to sit on her zafu for a full stick of
incense Diane expected the total of forty minutes. So Diane
was furious on hearing that Ziegler's daughter was having
an affair with the "master." Under no condition should a
teacher have sexual relations with a student. Diane was
vehement about this.

Sunderson could see that he would be regarded by the
group with strong suspicion. Mona had expressed interest
in joining the group so she could hang around there more,
and suggested that she volunteer his services as a janitor in
the church basement, fortunately pretty well soundproofed,
where they met. Everything was organized around volunteer
work but Americans aren't enthused about the janitorial so

it would be easy for her to get her "uncle interested in Zen" in as the group's janitor.

The master himself was to be called "Sky Blast," his idea, and he came from San Francisco. He appeared one day in Ann Arbor, supposedly to visit an old girlfriend, and took up wearing his traditional black robes around campus. Sky Blast also loved zoos and it was at the Detroit Zoo where he came upon his idea of howler monkeys to which we are related though not nearly so closely as to chimpanzees. The master's contention was that we were primates who began life howling. Mona was amused by this but found the howling unbearable compared with the traditional silence of meditation. Certain sopranos in the group were absolutely shattering. The howling was considered a privilege and on specific days only a few righteous students were allowed to howl and the others had to remain silent. There was one day of total silence per week and Mona wondered if they'd become suspicious if she attended only on those days. Security was taken to the utmost because early on there was an interloper who wrote a parodic exposé and played a recording of the howling when he was interviewed on a local radio station. Practice was early every morning after Margaret Ziegler served them a Tibetan breakfast. If you wanted to be holy no one could compete with Tibetans. Mona said the food was edible if you brought your own hot sauce. This was against the rules but members did it anyway.

During Mona's first dokusan, a private meeting with Sky Blast, he had asked her to arrange her robes so he could see up under them. The same old, same old, she thought but did so out of a sense of humor. They were interrupted

by his lover Margaret, who glared at Mona's loose robes.
Mona noticed later that Margaret was still peeved when
she demanded that Mona peel extra potatoes for the com-
munal dinner. Sky Blast said that he had been mourning
for Tibetan refugees and needed to see bare thighs to save
his spirits. He got an eyeful as Mona rarely wore undies.
After that he managed to brush up against her suggestively
several times. Ziegler's son, Michael, was obviously the lout
of the group. His sister had to keep an eye on him or he
would drink schnapps.

Sunderson reported in to Ziegler, limiting what he had
to say, and told him of the plan to infiltrate. Ziegler was
anxious and wanted him to drive down that evening but
Sunderson was tired and had a plan with Barbara early
the next morning. The first and last sex with her hopefully
would be memorable.

Marion had returned during his phone call with Mona
and chuckled incredulously when Sunderson filled him in.
They had caught six fish in all and drove hastily home and
made a fish chowder with potatoes, salt pork, and onions.
You poached the fish first to have a stock. Diane usually
served it with a pat of butter on top and then you watched
it melt patiently. You rounded it out with some half-and-half
and a dash of Tabasco.

They watched part of a pro football game but it was
dreary and low scoring and they were drowsy so they made
it an early night.

Weather permitting Barbara intended to come over
early in the morning to weed and Sunderson spent a restless night brooding about Marion's lecture and his morning

plans. He wasn't quite sure he could say to himself that sex was over for this short life. He was okay when he was still married to Diane but cutting that cord he became a nutcase. Could he deny himself beauty? Of course. Jail or prison would be particularly unpleasant for an ex-lawman.

Nevertheless, as agreed he left the back porch door unlocked for Barbara then waited all night for the click with a mixture of dread and anticipation. First he heard her pull up on her bicycle then walk softly and slowly up the stairs. She stood in his open doorway, smiled, and pulled off a sweatshirt and down with the shorts. Now she was nude. She sat gently on his bare chest and said, "This little bear went to market," and tickled his penis with her bare hand. She leaned over and gave him a rough French kiss, straddled his cock, and put it all the way in with a gasp.

"I think I love you more than my boyfriend."

"Don't say that." He held her back by her elbows thinking that this wasn't necessarily a good thing. Marion's words drummed in his ears. "You better pick on someone your own age."

She rolled into a crunch. "Do me like a dog. I read that people did that."

His resistance folded. He was on her with particular gusto, thinking that he was the happiest man on earth for the time being. Her back was radically muscular from gymnastics and she revolved herself below the waist aggressively. "Do that thing you did the first time on the sofa," she said. He knew she meant to go down on her which he did. She had a delightful whimper but then he heard the back gate of the garden open and Barbara's mother call out for her.

She was off the bed and deep into the closet in a trice. His heart hammered and he opened the window and answered. The upshot was that she was driving down the alley and had seen Barbara's bicycle at the back of his garden. Was she here? "No," he yelled. "She must have walked downtown with a friend. She's working here later." "Tell her to call when she shows up. Okay?" Barbara's mother continued down the alley in her blue Chevy. Barbara came out of the closet and laughed at his limp dick. "You aren't turned on by my mother?" She blew him then while giggling. "My boyfriend wants this every day. It gets boring." It worked and they returned to eating then dog style.

There was a very brief moment of shame, again a re-call of Marion's lecture. If it didn't stop now when he was sixty-six when did it stop? It couldn't continue, could it? In Blake's terms what are the actual limits of desire? He had no philological knowledge of what constitutes it. After the prom in high school his date Missy Carling had fallen asleep drunk on a friend's floor and he had shamefully lifted her frilly prom dress for a look. They were steady dates but other than simple kissing she wouldn't allow a touch, and he couldn't help thinking if he were still the star linebacker and not a lowly wrestler she'd feel differently. When swim-ming they would wrestle a little but the water diminished the sexuality of the act while lifting her dress was explosive, even more so than the tight swimsuit photos of Janet Leigh in *Life* magazine which had him chewing his fingers painfully. Once after a workout he was resting on a wrestling mat and Missy stood over his head in her scanty cheerleader outfit. He was keenly aware of her exposed body in all of its glory. As a senior she had abandoned him in favor of the star basketball player who had taken the team to the state semifinals. This made him burn with rage. He got in a fight with the guy who was unfortunately tough. The coach made them put on big, puffy sixteen-ounce gloves. The fight was declared a tie when Sunderson had hit him in the gut until he puked on the sidewalk outside the gym door. Missy watched the fight and was so disgusted she said she would never speak to him again, and she didn't until graduation day when she gave him a French kiss and said that he had always been the best kisser. She went off in the fall to Brown University on a big scholarship and ended up marrying a rich guy which had always been her ambition as the daughter of a poor biology teacher. The wedding was in Marquette but he hadn't been invited, he thought because he was at Michigan State. The basketball player was invited but then he went to the University of Michigan which was thought to be a step up and played star quality basketball there.

More than forty-five years later his temples still burned at the memory of lifting her prom dress. Lust didn't seem to go away. According to Marion, the curdled lust for Missy was still haunting him. You could feel practically sick with it. He had with Barbara wearing the T-shirt and sliding it up so that the prime rump was on display. That was as tough on his system as the time he'd made love with Mona in Paris. It was right after the rock 'n' roller left her for the young girls and Sunderson had been overwhelmed by her advances, he told himself. Diane had been angry but had eventually forgiven him because she knew Mona had used every hook and crook to seduce him and when it came to sex nearly all men were fools, him especially, which she'd learned from his slavish sexuality in their marriage. Now sexually sated with Barbara he, of course, could think of giving up sex with her.

He did however feel a remote tickle over the idea of anal sex, which he'd read about but done only once in college. According to his reading Brazilian girls considered it a birth control measure. But what if he were careless with Barbara and they ended up at the ER with a Beethoven chorus singing shame before a squad of police showed up?

He shivered and turned Barbara over on her belly. "Don't even think about it," he said to himself. He put the tip of his cock there.

"Don't even think about it," she said. "This coach over in Duluth did it there to a girl. She ended up going to a hospital that night. Think of explaining that to my parents. The coach had five kids and went to the same Catholic church as the girl's family. My aunt goes there and told me."

The story hit uncomfortably close to home. He asked what happened. "Nothing," she said. "They prayed a lot over her sore butt with the priest."

"What would your dad do?"

"Get out his deer rifle. He's real religious. He would shoot you square in the head, that's for sure. I might try it tomorrow with lots of lotion."

Sunderson was back to thinking of the seven deadly sins with the help of her dad's rifle. He wasn't coming close to her tomorrow. He'd be on a long hike in the woods if he could pick up a true friend from the dog pound.

It was noon and they were famished when they go out of bed, him with an aching prostate gland. He made them hamburgers from frozen patties, not a preference but all he had on hand.

"Fucking makes you real hungry," she said nonchalantly. They dozed on the sofa for fifteen minutes and then she went out and attacked her weeding. She despised the man Sunderson was working for and referred to his daughters as "rich bitches" and their brother as a "nerd" and a "dweeb," slang he wasn't familiar with. Later she took a shower and had a quarrelsome call with her mother concluding, "No I am not dressed properly. I'm showing Mr. Sunderson my bare ass. Old men like to look at bare asses." She slammed the phone down. "With Mother everything is propriety. Though my wicked aunt told me bawdy stories about her when she was in high school. Evidently she fucked the football coach on a junior camping trip."

Later that afternoon Sunderson made a trip to the grocery for some Stouffer's mac and cheese of which he always ate two packages, and then at the bar he ran into an old friend and his family sitting in the corner with a menu for the Italian place down the street trying to figure out if they could afford dinner. This embarrassed Sunderson with his ample pension and secret money from blackmailing the rock 'n' roller's rich mother. He supposedly saved the kid from a sex abuse charge for which he had received fifty grand. Little did she know that the charge she paid to protect him from was just a mixture of rumors a college friend at the LAPD had told him. They had been watching the rock musician hard but didn't have anything that would stick. And here Sunderson was chasing his tail about sex while millions were unemployed including his friend. His educated wife worked checkout at the supermarket while he was one of a legion of out of work computer programmers and a fine angler. Their son Billy had Down syndrome but their daughter Wendy was a straight-A student headed in the fall to Kalamazoo College on a big scholarship. When Billy saw Sunderson he brayed and aimed his finger around the room shouting *bang-bang* in honor of Sunderson's former profession. His sister calmed him down. Sunderson lied and said he had just won two hundred bucks in the lottery and wanted some greaseball lasagna so let's all go to dinner. He could tell that the mother didn't believe him but everyone was suddenly happy. He had a quick double and off they went. It was a chilly evening and he had a sense of winter approaching although the day had been pleasant.

Later that evening with considerable prostate discomfort he called another fishing friend who was a doctor. He told Sunderson to stop fucking so much. Sunderson lamely replied that he didn't know you could fuck too much. At dinner he had sat next to the attractive, flirtatious daughter and managed to get excited and sighed in despair. She was the daughter of a friend, he reminded himself. He slept poorly that night waking again and again to Barbara's delightful odor on the bedclothes. He thought over and over of his teen desire to become a Maori warrior in New Zealand where there was also a great supply of brown trout. By morning he had decided to control his obsessions by traveling more, even to New York City again to spend a week at the Museum of Natural History

with several trips to Katz's delicatessen. When he was growing up his father would occasionally make him Jewish-style
pickled tongue in a stone crock which he loved.

He decided to fly to Ann Arbor and rent a car, rather
than make the laborious drive, and soak his wealthy client
with the expense. He didn't want to face the airport twice
so he bought a one-way ticket and thought he'd go fishing
on the way back. He arranged to meet Mona at Zingerman's
where he always had a brisket sandwich with extra hot
horseradish, an inevitable gut bomb but sacrifices must be
made. Mona proudly announced she had bought him a pile
of used janitorial supplies at a yard sale. A man must have
a professional mop. That morning Barbara had dropped by
for what she called a "quickie" which his prostate scarcely
needed. He suspected that her athletic abilities promoted
her sexual energy. He would need a long trip to simply
recover.

He checked into a small suite at the Campus Inn where
he slept twenty minutes to handle his sandwich, then drove
over to the church basement to unload the supplies of his
new craft. There were long neat rows of zafus and zabu-
tons, Zen sitting cushions that Sunderson thought very uncomfortable. He had sat on the one Diane owned that she
kept stored in a closet and had fallen crudely off to the side
which meant to him that he wasn't built for meditation. They
packed the janitor stuff in a coat closet. Sky Blast and the
Ziegler girl came in the basement door with her carrying
a heavy load of groceries. He wasn't the grocery-carrying
type and wore a look of seedy reverence in his black robe,
the slack look of "Isn't life wonderful" that one sees in nickel

orientalists to whom the universe is a spiritual playground. Mona introduced them.

"We can afford to pay you very little."

"I'm volunteering because of my curiosity about Zen. My ex-wife was a practioner and it seemed to do her a lot of good."

Sky Blast looked at him with a trace of cynicism then let out with a shattering howler monkey screech that startled Sunderson witless. He was answered by Margaret in the kitchen who was equally loud.

"We are cleansing the dead air," Sky Blast announced with pretension. Sunderson went into the kitchen to help Margaret unpack the groceries. She was a big girl with a reasonably shaped fanny. It was strictly vegetarian stuff with lots of fruit, vegetables, juice, and not a trace of the pork sausage he valued so highly. There were also big bags of a Tibetan cereal called tsampa. He would have to make his own breakfast before he came to work. Michael Ziegler the lout was making eyes at Mona, who regarded him as one does a dog turd.

"What are you doing?" Sky Blast barked.

"Helping with the groceries."

"That's women's work," he said.

Margaret served them a cup of tea at an aluminum table. Sky Blast had seemed to notice Sunderson's glance at her butt.

"You may find my approach to zazen a bit unorthodox but I received a dispensation on the top of Mount Tamalpais last year that our age will be undergoing a resurgence of the natural world in our time. Howler monkeys are our primate predecessors. We must honor them. I am fascinated by the oneness of all living things."

"Me too," said Sunderson for lack of anything else to say.

"Good. Then we'll get along. Call me Roshi Sky."

"Fine by me, Roshi Sky."

"See you at five tomorrow morning."

Sunderson wasn't enthused about getting up that early except to go fishing though he rather looked forward to howling like a monkey. People of this ilk kept trying to help you "get in touch with yourself." He wasn't at all sure that this was a pleasant idea though he knew in his heart that he had to put a stop to things with Barbara however late in the game it was. He vowed as punishment that he would have to go to that mind doctor if he screwed her again. Cross my heart, hope to die, stick a needle in my eye, they used to say.

He was up before daylight and fried two good-sized sausage patties. He had read that mountain climbers were never vegetarians. Of course he had no intention of climbing mountains but he liked the solidity of the idea that pork rather than cereal could get you up Everest.

In the church basement the rows were three-quarters full of meditators and Sky Blast glowered at the late arrivals from the kitchen, finally making a mighty howl which the others joined. Sunderson started tentatively with not much more than a squeak. Sky Blast came up behind him and told him to use his lungs completely as if he were a monkey singing opera. He did so and found it oddly satisfying like yelling at his sister Berenice when he was young. As he glanced into the kitchen it occurred to him that Margaret must eat a lot of vegetables to get an ass that big. Down the

row her brother Michael's face seemed fixed permanently
in a smirk. He was a heavy cross for Margaret to carry.
Sunderson learned that he was a football player and allowed
to eat a big steak at a restaurant every night for dinner. He
was also the only man allowed to date outside the group.
His father had given him a new yellow Corvette for making
the team. He had a black girlfriend and would say loudly
that he preferred "dark meat."

Of all the howlers Sky Blast was the loudest, obviously
playing to his strength. Mona's voice was the most penetrating. It was high and clear and if there had been any actual
animals in the area they would be frightened witless. Late-
comers said that even with the soundproofing any strays or
dogs being walked fled the area posthaste. When Sunderson
was a child he was friends with a local Ojibwa family and
once at a powwow they asked him to join in their chanting
and singing. He recalled what a wonderful sensation it was
to chant at drumbeats during a full moon in August. There
were northern lights that evening which made it even more
eerie. His friend's father told him that the song they had
sung was about summer waning in August. The next dawn
he and his friend went out and caught a big pail of bluegills
and perch and there was breakfast around the campfire of
fried fish cooked in massive iron skillets. He had a crush on
a pretty Indian girl who thoroughly ignored him except once
were they were playing hide-and-seek and in the woods she
kissed him impulsively.

As they continued to yodel in the church basement he
noted that Michael stared at Mona with graceless lust, not
that he could blame him. She was by far the prettiest girl

in the group. When they finished their howling they sat in silence for a full stick of incense, forty minutes, a tip of the hat to tradition. They had a predictably awful breakfast. His legs hurt mightily from his attempt to keep balance on the zafu. The tsampa tasted like cattle feed and didn't help his pain. His prospects with these nitwits looked glum.

On the way back to the hotel Mona and Sunderson decided to pick up brisket and horseradish sandwiches, so they took a long slow walk to Zingerman's. He dreaded calling Ziegler. He didn't want a phone call to ruin his meaty sandwich, the surging track of protein he desperately needed.

Back in the room Mona laid out their lunch. Even the pickle and potato salad were wondrous. Mona stripped to her undies which was discomfiting, saying she didn't want the juice from hers to drip on her clean clothes. He got an instant hard-on despite his recent hard work with Barbara. They had been amused on the way home to see Sky Blast sneaking out the back door of a hamburger joint with a package and cramming a big bite right there in the alley. Sky Blast hadn't seen them and Sunderson was not without sympathy for the sneaky vegetarian.

He had a small whiskey for courage before he dialed Ziegler. He reminded himself that the man was a hothead but he himself would quit before he took any shit or abuse. The conversation started poorly with Sunderson admitting that Ziegler's daughter was "living in sin" with Sky Blast. Ziegler went off like a roaring rocket saying abruptly, "My poor baby." Sunderson was somewhat mystified. How many friends even when he was active as a detective would say they would kill anyone who fooled with their daughter?

ɔons were home free and if they were seducers the father would brag, "My son gets more ass than a toilet seat." A mystery, all of it. They wanted a daughter to stay "daddy's little girl," though frequently they ignored her. Sunderson's only firsthand experience of father-daughter relationships, of course, was Mona, so perhaps it was better not to think about it. He noticed both Michael and Margaret's sister had told Ziegler nothing, obviously wanting their dad to stay out of their lives.

He had seen Sky Blast and Michael practicing wrestling holds out in the lobby. They were both big men, well over six feet and quite obviously muscular. It turned out they had been high school and college wrestlers. Michael was thicker and a bit stronger but Sky Blast was deft and extremely fast. Sunderson bet in an all-out fight Sky Blast's speed could win if he could avoid Michael getting him in a choke hold which was the finish of any fight. Sunderson's father had taught him early in high school that since he wasn't a fast puncher he would be better off learning a good gut punch, knowledge he made use of against the basketball player. This was because if you knocked out an opponent's wind he couldn't continue. It was such a ghastly feeling that he was immediately a wounded puppy. The current wrestle seemed anti-Zen to him but boys would be boys he supposed.

Sunderson left Ann Arbor by car early the next morning telling Mona to tell Sky Blast that his mother was mortally ill. She said she would sweep up and mop the mud tracked from the churchyard. He called Ziegler from Clare and told him he would meet him for drinks in Trenary at five o'clock. That was fine Ziegler said because they were unlikely to see anyone they knew in Trenary.

Sunderson had a case of "lover's nuts," scrotal discomfort caused by his great moral victory before he left. He had been careful not to drink too much at dinner because he knew he might lose control. He suspected that Mona would try to seduce him. She did. She slept on the couch which opened into a bed and it took her quite a while to accept the fact that he wasn't going to close the deal. She was bouncing naked on the bed and tried to sit on his hard-on. He rolled off the bed, quickly dressed, and went down to the front desk for another room giving the concierge strict instructions not to tell her where he was. He had a double whiskey out of a pint in his luggage which didn't help. He watched an old Vincent Price movie where a killer was sabotaging parachuters' chutes.

They had a hurried breakfast in her room the next morning with Mona only in her undies. She sprawled obscenely with her bagel but was also disconsolate.

"Mona, I'm like your father. It's out of the question."

"I don't need a father. I got a letter from my real father this week. He wants me to visit him in Los Angeles. My mother has remarried and doesn't want anything to do with me."

Sunderson sat there with an English muffin and an indelicate hard-on, quarreling with his own mind. He frankly felt cheap but if one more session got to Diane everything would be over with her. He suddenly ran from the room, took the elevator, and was out in the parking lot in a trice. He had forgotten his suitcase but Mona could send it. He hoped Mona's father wouldn't break her heart again.

He made the bar in Trenary in six tiresome hours and had a couple of doubles as he waited for Ziegler half an hour.

Ziegler's tantrum was immediate. He had talked to his son who had obviously finally spilled the beans about what was going on in Ann Arbor. He knew it was all reprehensible in his father's terms and had wanted to keep his sister's secrets, but his wrangling with Sky Blast had given him a taste for revenge. The bartender came out to the bar porch to see what the yelling was about so Sunderson gestured Ziegler down the street. In his braying voice Ziegler offered Sunderson a $5,000 bonus if he would retrieve his daughter from Ann Arbor.

"Can't do it. She's over eighteen and that would be the serious felony of kidnap."

"But she's my fucking daughter," Ziegler wailed. "I can't give her up to a fucking California hippie. She was dating a quarterback a few months ago."

Sunderson said nothing, reflecting on how many parents think that they virtually own their children. The children are never allowed to become independent beings.

Ziegler bellowed, "You chickenshit. You're fired. I'll fucking get her myself." Ziegler ran for his car and swerved off in the other direction from home.

Well, it made the next morning's *Detroit Free Press* in a big way. Pure mayhem. Sunderson caught up with it over breakfast at a local eatery, having returned to an empty pantry. Evidently Ziegler, the ex–University of Michigan football star, was the paper implied a very rough customer. According to Ziegler's daughter Margaret her father and brother came into their house and immediately attacked "Mr.

Sky Blast, a Zen teacher from California. Sources revealed that Sky Blast's students howl like the primate howler monkeys during meditation which is unique to their sect. Mr. Sky Blast is also a trained martial arts champion specializing in judo. He defended himself capably from the attack and now all three are in the hospital. Margaret Ziegler reported that her brother hit Sky Blast in the face with a baseball bat. Ms. Ziegler called the police who quelled the fight with difficulty. Mr. Ziegler Senior is being charged with assault and resisting arrest in addition to other charges, including significant property damage to the apartment."

Sunderson's disgust was immediate and wholehearted. He didn't feel culpable but was ashamed that he had had anything to do with these people. He called the chief of police for Ann Arbor and gave a telephone statement to the effect that he had worked for Ziegler in his efforts to retrieve his daughter but had been recently fired after refusing to simply kidnap her. "Wise choice," the chief said. Sunderson had known him from long ago but had never liked him because of the man's essentially fascist attitudes about police work. The chief told Sunderson he might have to come back to Ann Arbor as the case developed.

Sunderson noticed a waitress who had a startling resemblance to Mona. He couldn't help staring, which started a long session of near nausea that lasted several hours. He knew he had to rid himself of his aimlessness and criminal activity, including Barbara. He called and asked her to meet him on his back porch in an hour. He chafed against the self-denial but he had to stop this sexual nonsense. He would have to become a hermit fisherman. Even in winter he could afford to go anywhere to fish. Both coasts of Mexico beckoned.

She arrived while he was having a stiff drink. She quickly made herself some lemonade on this crisp autumn day when the maples were sparkling in their multicolored beauty.

"It's over," he said to her.

"I was afraid you would say that. Just when I was really enjoying it."

"You can resume with someone your own age or a college boy."

"But I love you," she pouted.

"Don't say that. My friend the prosecutor said he had been tipped off. The paperboy saw us together in the living room and told his parents. They reported it. If I were charged I could get ten years for sexual abuse of a minor. I don't have that many years left and I can't bear the idea of spending them in prison. They'd love to convict an ex-detective." He felt a bit desperate lying to her but somehow believed it would let her down easier than a simple rejection.

"We could run away together."

"I've thought of it but there's no safe place."

As luck would have it Barbara's parents, Bruce and Ellen, came driving down the alley in their boring beige Camry. Barbara waved and pulled the hem of her skirt down. She had worn an especially short one for his delectation. Bruce and Ellen came through the back garden gate. Barbara had stacked all of the autumn garden detritus near the gate for the garbage truck. Bruce looked coolly at the weeded garden.

"Nice job. You should do this at home."

Sunderson got up to shake hands and offered a drink. Bruce was small and had a slightly nasty edge known as the *small man's syndrome*.

"No thanks. I only drink after dark except in summer when the dark comes so late up here."

"What are you drinking dear? I hope it's not wine."

"Lemonade," Barbara said looking in her glass.

"Offer your mother some, dear," Sunderson said. It was evident that Barbara wasn't going to make a move to do so unless he said something.

They chatted like neighbors for a few minutes and then Bruce and Ellen were off for the store. When they left Barbara burst into tears again then went through the house to catch the last of the autumn sun on the front porch.

"I don't see how you can leave me high and dry when I love you." She started sobbing as he looked at her wonderful legs thinking that they should be around his neck. He had poured a huge drink when they walked through the house hoping it would make him calm and meditative. No such luck. He felt a flood of warm tears. The local paper had called repeatedly about the Ann Arbor violence. He hadn't answered.

Suddenly she was running down the street toward home still sobbing. He felt more interior tears then saw her dreaded parents coming down the street in their Camry back from the short grocery trip. He waved, they waved. He felt light-headed from his first moral choice in recent memory though part of his motive was not to be in prison for the opening of trout season next spring. There was a virtual flash in his mind of Barbara's gorgeous bare butt but he was undeterred. He already felt and was trying to subdue his regret. Good people don't have it easy, he reflected, though he wasn't really a good person.

It was a scant fifteen minutes before Barbara's mother was doing a military march down the street toward him. He was happy he had refreshed his drink.

"My daughter is sobbing. I think it's about you. Did you fire her?"

"No I didn't fire her. She's just starting to trim the hedges. She was unhappy this morning about something."

"Well she seems to be sobbing about you. If her father finds out you're up to something with her you'll go straight to prison."

She turned around and marched up the street.

Sunderson felt sweat oozing from every pore though the air was cool. He went inside and refreshed his drink yet again. He was tempted to cut and run for his trout cabin, but it was only two days from deer season when the orange army would invade the north. He called Marion anyway. They usually opened the season without much interest at his cabin. But as the phone rang with no answer he remembered that Marion was in Hawaii with his wife for a big indigenous conference. Everyone in the Midwest except Sunderson wanted to go to Hawaii, though it interested him slightly more thinking about it having its own native population. There was the idea that he should move to a remote place out of harm's way. Early in his detective career he would have been happy indeed to bust someone for his current behavior. It would likely bring a ten-year sentence.

Now his sweat turned cold and even more ample. He went in, poured yet another drink, and then pushed it aside and gathered his gear for a cold trip to the cabin. There were snow flurries already up there though the weather report hadn't predicted anything dire. Winter was coming on so quickly. He packed his rifle and shells in order to at least pretend he was deer hunting. He had long ago lost his taste for it so cherished when he was a teenager and they got the first few days of deer season off school. He prized the memory of shooting a big buck near town when he was sixteen. It dressed out at two hundred pounds and those were hard times. His dad had shot a little spikehorn but Sunderson proudly delivered a real hunk of meat for the family. Like many northern folks they all loved venison and his mother regularly made a stew out of the lesser bits with a big lard crust on top he adored that soaked up the gravy. There was also a nice corn relish a cousin sent up from Indiana. It was virtually impossible to grow sweet corn in Munising or Grand Marais.

He went to bed early very drunk and woke up for the trip very hungover. He couldn't make it past a single piece of toast. On the way out of town he would pick up a few steaks and a dozen pasties. While he was packing the car Barbara rode past on her bicycle on the way to school, the tenth grade he reminded himself with self-loathing.

"I got time for a quickie if you like," she said, getting off her bike and revealing her winsome crotch.

"I'm too hungover," he said feeling his bilge rising. She ignored this, walked into his house, and leaned over the kitchen table lifting her skirt and dropping her panties to the ankles. He couldn't resist and then off she went whistling her way to school. He was suddenly exhausted and sat on the sofa reading the morning *Detroit Free Press* that had been delivered by the mouthy paperboy.

He was pleased to read in a longish article that the former football hero Ziegler was being charged with both assault and illegal entry. He paid fines to get out of the rest but his daughter Margaret, the legal tenant, had refused to open the door, or so she testified, saying that Ziegler and her brother saw Sky Blast standing behind her and broke down the front door. Ziegler threw the first punches, a critical matter in charging him, and Michael grazed him in the head with a bat, but Sky Blast was in fine shape with some martial arts training. Margaret knocked her brother over the head with a rolling pin which turned the tide as he had Sky Blast in a sometimes fatal choke hold from behind. Margaret had called the police and when they arrived Sky Blast was busy throwing both father and son off the front porch. All were arrested. Ziegler was a bloody mess from face punches and Michael had a minor skull fracture for which he would never forgive his sister. Sky Blast was put in a cast for a broken arm and knuckles but had clearly defended himself well against the two big bullies.

The real news was that a small town cop in the Bay Area of San Francisco had been surfing the Net and recognized Sky Blast's photo as that of a man known locally as Roshi Simmons who had an open arrest warrant for embezzling a large amount of money from a Bay Area Buddhist organization. Extradition orders were being filed. So Sky Blast had feet of clay, Sunderson thought, a little embarrassed by his amusement. Ziegler would be happy about that no matter how badly he and his pride were injured.

Sunderson felt mildly suicidal, a new emotion for him as the least self-judgmental person imaginable. He had not been able to resist Barbara once, even looking at ten in the hoosegow. He decided to put off his departure one more day, wondering at the absurd mystery of love and lust and his own questionable behavior in the face of them. Helpless in the world, he thought. None of the pretty girls were available to him in high school so maybe he was living the unlived life. He knew even as he thought it that it was a lie. He'd never unlived life. Without Diane divorcing him none of this could have happened, starting with Mona. But his dad used to say, "No excuses" and there really weren't any in this case. You walk away from something wrong in an ideal world. He hadn't done so.

He was sure he had loved Diane during their more than twenty-five years of marriage. He had fucked up the whole thing with drinking and talking ad nauseam about the grim aspects of his work as a detective for the state police, the many wife and child beatings and sexually abused children. She simply couldn't bear that dose of reality and it was sadistic of him to unburden himself because he couldn't bear it either. The culture said it was very wrong to make love to his fifteen-year-old gardener. Making love to the married neighbor lady was not recommended either but was at least legal.

He awoke at 7:00 a.m. to an unpleasant call from Ziegler who demanded he drive to Ann Arbor and pick up Margaret.

"Have you forgotten you fired me?" Sunderson replied.

"You're hired again. Go get her pronto."

"Fuck you big shot." Sunderson hung up on him.

The second call, to his cell, was far worse. It was his quasi-friend the prosecutor. He explained in painful detail that Barbara's parents had taken her to a female shrink, new in town, and she had told her everything about her affair with Sunderson.

"She's lying," Sunderson said impulsively.

"Doesn't sound like it," the prosecutor said. "You got your ass in a sling. Come in to see me this morning." He knew the prosecutor was bending the rules in that he hadn't yet been arrested.

"I can't. I'm at my cabin deer hunting."

"I'll give you until Friday. That's four days. Be here. I don't want to have to get a warrant and have you picked up."

"Thank you," Sunderson said. He hung up, then went into the toilet and puked up breakfast. Except for drinking, he hadn't vomited since a bad case of Asian flu twenty years before. This was a special occasion.

He drove off for the cabin feeling as if he weighed nothing in the front seat of the car. He pulled off in an empty restaurant parking lot on the way west of town and called the bartender near the cabin, who looked after the place for him, to warn of his arrival. His mind was naturally jumbled and totally out of focus. He thought of Brazil but was not sure he was ready for such a foreign lifestyle. His other option was Nogales, Mexico, right across the border which he knew only required a driver's license though they were becoming stricter. But then again there was no real fishing around Nogales except pond catfish. Brazil would be the safest place as they wouldn't extradite him but whoever heard of jungle trout. The poignant fear was that if he went to prison at sixty-six years of age he likely wouldn't get out until age seventy-six and by then he'd probably be too weak to fish and wade swift rivers. This put both stomach and brain in an ugly turmoil. What did he have in mind whazzing mere girls? Simple dumb lust whatever that was. He couldn't pin it down. It was like a stomachache you never get rid of from age twelve to seventy-plus possibly.

There was a dusting of powder snow on the long two track from the main road back to the cabin. He wasn't worried if it really came down, as they had instructions at the tavern to come tow him out if necessary. He had fenced about five acres around the cabin with barbed wire and watered the ground well from a pump next to the river. Despite the fence there were deer prints everywhere and evidence they'd dug down to green grass. It was beautiful to watch deer jump fences. They rarely failed and would right themselves with a somersault if their back legs didn't quite make it.

The cabin was warm and cozy with a small fire in the fireplace started by the bartender and a nice stack of dry wood. He noticed that the television was missing, either thieved or borrowed, but he wasn't concerned. Occasionally a local hermit, or so he thought, would break in and heat up a can of beans but would clean up after himself.

He poured a modest drink and sat in an easy chair staring at his beloved river. He had vowed to drink moderately in order to get up early and hunt if he so chose. Despite his happiness over where he was he could not lessen the knot in his stomach over fear of prison and missing ten years of trout fishing. It was unacceptable in his last years but what were the options? Facing the music, they called it. He would also miss the spring bird chatter he prized. If Barbara had told the counselor everything the woman was obliged to go to the prosecutor with this crime. The sex had certainly been consensual but that was irrelevant given her age. He was plainly and fatally cornered. He didn't much care about the public shame though he was relieved that at least his mother was dead and wouldn't endure the humiliation.

He grieved over the fact that Diane would have to see how low he had stooped. Also his only real friend Marion who had warned him to "grow up" and "pick on women his own age."

The bartender, Eddie, came out with the television saying his own was on the blink and his kids howled over missing it. Sunderson said that he only needed it for two more days and then Eddie could have it. Eddie was delighted and Sunderson added that he was going to buy himself a small television that he had to squint at to discourage watching so much news. This was beyond Eddie's comprehension but his thanks were profuse. Eddie said he rarely got more than a quarter tip at the bar.

Sunderson fried up a good rare rib steak with a glass of mediocre red that hadn't survived very well after six weeks in the refrigerator though he judged it drinkable if barely. He stoked up the fireplace with two good-sized maple logs knowing he'd be up by 4:00 a.m. to add wood.

He had a horrid and exhausting night with only intermittent dozing. He remembered his youth when it was

impossible to sleep the night before deer opening. That
wasn't it this time. It was the prospective prison sentence,
if not ten then at least seven years. He kept waking from
vivid dreams of trying to fly-cast in the bone dry Jackson
prison yard. His stomach knotted and he got up several
times for a shot of whiskey. He thought that most people
sent to prison had nothing to do except commit more
crimes. He had to think he was different, but maybe that
was just false hope. How could the law consign his final
years to prison when he needed trout fishing to live? The
local judge was a hanging judge in sex cases, a devout
Baptist who thought sexuality was verminous. He could
expect no mercy from that quarter. Diane might offer to
help pay for a lawyer, but he viewed it as a waste of her
money. Deep in the night watching the fireplace flicker
he knew very well he was doomed. An open-and-shut
case. Goodbye river. Maybe he would die on a prison cot
as if it mattered. They had a special section for feloni-
ous lawmen but what did that matter? It saved you from
being murdered by other inmates when you probably no
longer much cared.

   He gave up trying to sleep at 5:00 a.m. It was hopeless now that he had seen his future totally disappear. He
got up, stirred the fire into a warm blaze. He was taking
part in the ancient but senseless art of deer hunting. On
opening day you got up and breakfasted very early and
then sat around a couple of hours talking and waiting for
daylight. He could remember dozing at the table while
his father and friends talked relentlessly about the hunts
of the past.

Sunderson made a pan of fried spuds, a pan of sausage, and four scrambled eggs wishing he had a dog to share the bounty. In the first pale light he saw a large buck near the edge of the fence and the river. He could have tilted a window open and shot it but he felt pretty good and didn't want to start the day with a cheap move. That could come later if necessary. He ate most of his breakfast and left the rest out for visiting coyotes along with last night's steak bone.

He heard shots from not that far north on the river. He could see clearly now because the light was growing stronger. A small button buck, so called because its horns were mere nubbins and had not yet grown into a spike horn, failed to clear the fence, three strands of barbed wire where it was loose near the cabin. The button buck failed the jump and became horribly entangled in the barbed wire. Sunderson cussed and took his combination pliers and wire cutters out with him in his flimsy summer robe. According to the thermometer it was near zero and his feet were cold. The deer was a mere boy but lashed out at him furiously with its sharp hooves so that he couldn't get close enough to cut it out of the entanglement. It was hopeless indeed and the little deer was cutting itself witlessly on the sharp barbs. Sunderson cursed and vowed to cut down the meaningless fence that day. Why give a fuck about his yard at the cabin when he didn't care at home? The deer got more entangled and Sunderson went inside and got his rifle, the only possible solution. He shot the boy in the heart but hated it to be the deer's last memory of earth. He spontaneously turned the rifle barrel on himself, feeling the coldness against his forehead. He moved the barrel upward a ways because he didn't want to make a mess but not so far upward it would only be a grazing shot. He pulled the trigger and fell beside the dead deer. In his mind he was fishing a river and his lovely ex-wife was sitting on the bank with their picnic basket reading a book as usual.